D1592868

Rough Ride

Also from Kristen Ashley

Rough Ride

A Chaos Novella

By Kristen Ashley

1001 Dark Nights

EVIL EYE
CONCEPTS

Rough Ride
A Chaos Novella
By Kristen Ashley

1001 Dark Nights

Copyright 2018 Kristen Ashley
ISBN: 978-1-945920-93-6

Foreword: Copyright 2014 M. J. Rose

Published by Evil Eye Concepts, Incorporated

Acknowledgments from the Author

Thank you to Liz Berry and MJ Rose for having this phenomenal idea of banding the sisterhood (and brotherhood) of romance novelists together for the benefit of many, giving us the chance to tell these stories, and support our sistren and brethren with theirs.

And more gratitude for honoring me by asking me to be a part of it.

Dedication

To Hellen Kirina Fernandez
A true beauty inside and out.
A true warrior.
A true inspiration.

Thank God you read my books.
If you had not, I would never have had
the pleasure of meeting you.

Sign up for the 1001 Dark Nights Newsletter
and be entered to win a Tiffany Key necklace.

There's a contest every month!

Go to www.1001DarkNights.com to subscribe.

As a bonus, all subscribers will receive a free copy of
Discovery Bundle Three
Featuring stories by
Sidney Bristol, Darcy Burke, T. Gephart
Stacey Kennedy, Adriana Locke
JB Salsbury, and Erika Wilde

One Thousand and One Dark Nights

Once upon a time, in the future...

*I was a student fascinated with stories and learning.
I studied philosophy, poetry, history, the occult, and
the art and science of love and magic. I had a vast
library at my father's home and collected thousands
of volumes of fantastic tales.*

*I learned all about ancient races and bygone
times. About myths and legends and dreams of all
people through the millennium. And the more I read
the stronger my imagination grew until I discovered
that I was able to travel into the stories... to actually
become part of them.*

*I wish I could say that I listened to my teacher
and respected my gift, as I ought to have. If I had, I
would not be telling you this tale now.
But I was foolhardy and confused, showing off
with bravery.*

*One afternoon, curious about the myth of the
Arabian Nights, I traveled back to ancient Persia to
see for myself if it was true that every day Shahryar
(Persian: شهريار, "king") married a new virgin, and then
sent yesterday's wife to be beheaded. It was written
and I had read, that by the time he met Scheherazade,
the vizier's daughter, he'd killed one thousand
women.*

Something went wrong with my efforts. I arrived in the midst of the story and somehow exchanged places with Scheherazade – a phenomena that had never occurred before and that still to this day, I cannot explain.

Now I am trapped in that ancient past. I have taken on Scheherazade's life and the only way I can protect myself and stay alive is to do what she did to protect herself and stay alive.

Every night the King calls for me and listens as I spin tales. And when the evening ends and dawn breaks, I stop at a point that leaves him breathless and yearning for more. And so the King spares my life for one more day, so that he might hear the rest of my dark tale.

As soon as I finish a story... I begin a new one... like the one that you, dear reader, have before you now.

Prologue

Hurt

Rosalie

He spit on me.

I felt it land on the side of my chin and slide down.

I didn't move to wipe it away.

I couldn't.

Lying on my side, curled into a ball, the pain screamed through me. All of it—and there was a lot of it—demanding attention, I couldn't concentrate, couldn't think, couldn't move in case it got worse. I couldn't do anything but lie there and pray that it was over.

It wasn't.

He bent over me, grabbed my hair, yanked it back, and I felt his hot breath hit my face.

"See if he wants you now, you stupid bitch," he hissed.

He let my hair go and I felt him retreat, but he still wasn't done.

He kicked me so hard with his foot in its heavy motorcycle boot, my body slid across the cement.

I was too far gone even to grunt.

I felt something bounce off my hip, clatter to the floor, and then his voice came back, this time from further away.

"There you go, baby," he drawled. "Your line to Chaos. We're done with you. *I'm* done with you. Now they can have you."

I heard boots on cement, more than just his, his Bounty brothers in the club. I sustained a couple more kicks as they passed. One of them grabbed the underside of my jaw and shoved my head back into the cement, also spitting, his hitting my neck.

And then they were gone.

I lay there, my focus on breathing and continuing to do it even though each breath was not only an effort but an agony. The fear I'd felt early when he took me, how he'd taken me, the way he'd handled me and I knew he'd figured it out, had dissipated as pain took its place. Now, the fear was returning that they'd come back and dish out more.

He'd come back.

Throttle.

No, to me he was Beck. My boyfriend. Gerard Beck. He hated the first name Gerard so everyone called him Beck. All his life. Or since he could demand that happen and not allow anything but that. Even his mother called him Beck.

Until he got his club name, Throttle. All his brothers called him that. When I was with him when he was with his brothers, I also called him that.

But when we were alone, at home, he was Beck.

My Beck.

My man. My lover. My protector. My future.

The man who'd just spit on me and kicked me.

But he'd done more before that.

He'd grabbed me from work and delivered me right to them, right to where I was right then. Even starting it, choking me until I thought I'd blank out, then clocking me in the temple, then on the jaw, then on my cheekbone.

Throttle.

That name was given to him for a reason but not the reason he'd now become Throttle to me.

I shut my eyes tight, opened them, reached to the phone he'd tossed at me and endured the immense pain that scoured through me, leaving me feeling even more raw, which if my brain had room to process anything further, I would have thought unimaginable.

My fingers closed around the phone and I huffed out little breaths, which were hard to take since each one sent fire through my midsection. So I tried deep breaths, and those were worse because the fire lasted even longer.

Dread intermingled with all the rest as I tried to focus on moving my thumb to open the phone, but I saw the black creeping in at the sides of my eyes.

I couldn't pass out.

I had to call for help.

I had to get out of there.

My body had different ideas, sending the message to my brain that this was too much, it couldn't take more.

So I passed out.

* * * * *

I came to woozy and disoriented.

The pain, the stench of the room, the feel of the cement beneath me brought it all slamming back, along with the panic.

Having no idea how long I was out, feeling the phone resting in my hand, I actually grunted with the effort of sliding it up, wrapping my fingers around it, using my thumb to flip it open.

An old-style flip phone.

A burner.

We'd joked about it, Snap and me. He'd called me Scully. He had a burner too, so there'd be no caller ID when he phoned me. So I'd called him Mulder.

I was going to call him.

Not because I was working for Chaos anymore. I wasn't. That officially ended on that cement. Definitely not because I was protecting Bounty. I'd tell the police. Absolutely, I'd tell the police my boyfriend's motorcycle club beat the snot out of me. It didn't matter that I broke the code, and knew it. It didn't matter that I'd betrayed my man, and done it deliberately.

I was trying to save him. Save his brothers. Save his club. Save everyone.

I closed my eyes tight, my thumb moving over the phone from memory, knowing the way on its own, I called him so often. That was why I was calling him now rather than 911. I knew how to get to him. To Snapper. And the effort would be less. I could dial the digits to get him up on speed dial in my sleep, so I could do it lying on a cement floor, beat to hell and practically unable to move.

I couldn't lift the phone to my ear so I just shoved it across the floor closer to my face, listening to it ring.

"Rosie?" Snap answered.

I closed my eyes tighter as understanding hit me with a blow almost as brutal as every strike I'd just taken.

God.

I hadn't done it to save Beck. To save his brothers, his club…everybody.

At first, I'd done it to make Beck into Shy.

And then I'd done it to make him be Snapper.

And last, I'd done it to make his club Chaos.

"Rosie?" Snap's Eddie Vedder baritone got sharper.

Oh no.

No.

The black was creeping in again.

"Sss…" was all I could get out.

"*Rosalie*," he bit out, curt, alert, *alarmed*.

"Hurt," I whispered.

And then, again, I blacked out.

* * * * *

I'd come to and gone out, managed to drag myself a few feet toward the door, hearing the burner ring, then stop, ring again, stop, drifting in and out before I heard him.

"Jesus, fuck, *Jesus, fuck*."

Snapper.

"Ambulance or call a brother?"

Roscoe.

"Rosie, honey, you with us?"

Snap, close to me, pulling my hair out of my face gently.

"Fuck," growled from Roscoe. "Those motherfuckers spit on her."

"Rosie, babe, darlin', you with us?"

Snap, tighter, letting the anger rise through the concern.

My eyelids fluttered.

"Good, honey, good, stay with us," Snapper ordered.

"Am-am…bu—" I tried.

"Okay, baby, okay, good," Snap cut me off, not making me expend more effort. Then to Roscoe, "Call an ambulance, man."

I felt hands on me, careful but not hesitant, swift and searching. Moans coasted out, little twitches when he'd hit a bad spot that sent new aches, stings, or fire through me.

"Gotta check, honey," Snap murmured apologetically while Roscoe talked on the phone somewhere else. "Stay awake, Rosie. Stay with me, yeah?"

I said nothing until I moaned again when I felt him gently lift my head then rest it on something that was a lot softer than cement.

It smelled of leather.

His Club cut.

I was lying on Chaos.

I swallowed.

It hurt.

Thankfully, Snapper quit his body injury survey and started stroking my hair.

That hurt too.

Roscoe came back. "Called emergency. Called Tack. Where we at with Rosalie?"

"Ribs, definitely. Right wrist is bad," Snapper told him, still stroking my hair.

"Face is a definite too," Roscoe said in an infuriated mutter.

Face too.

Oh yes.

They definitely took care of my face.

"Someone choked the fuck outta her," Roscoe kept up the tally, the fury in his voice escalating.

That wasn't a "they." That was only Beck.

"Was it Bounty?" Roscoe asked.

"Of course it was Bounty," Snapper stated tersely.

"We gotta know, brother," Roscoe returned quietly.

I felt his hand leave my hair, which was a relief, but then his fingers curled around mine, which made me wince.

Eightball had bent them so far back, it was a wonder they didn't snap off as he was holding me when he was hitting me.

"Squeeze once, it was Bounty, Rosie," Snap said.

I wasn't going to squeeze. It was easier to speak.

"Yeah," I pushed out.

"'Kay, babe, 'kay," he crooned, thankfully his fingers leaving mine, but they went back to my hair. "We got it now. You're good. Gonna take care of you."

No they weren't.

He wasn't.

No one was going to take care of me.

But me.

Not anymore.

They were supposed to do that before.

And now I was on a cement floor, beat to hell.

But I was going to be.

Good that was.

Yes, I was going to be.

Finally.

And it was going to be me that made me that too.

I turned my face into Snap's cut as an indication he shouldn't stroke my hair anymore, as a way to tell him to get the heck away from me, to leave me to the ambulance, to leave me alone, to get out of my hair, out of there, out of my *life*.

But the fabric snagged my swollen nose and a whimper slid from me.

"Baby," he whispered, feeling close, seemingly all around me, "just hang tight. Don't move. Help will be here soon."

Help would be there soon.

I'd be in an ambulance.

Then I'd be in a hospital.

While there, I'd talk to the police.

Eventually, I'd go home and live in fear of what my boyfriend's motorcycle club would do to me after I pressed charges against them for beating the crap out of me.

What could be worse than this?

I didn't know.

I didn't want to find out.

But there was a good possibility I would.

I couldn't think of that.

So instead I thought about the fact that I actually couldn't go home. I had to move out of the home I shared with Beck, but I could only do that after I figured out where the hell I'd go.

It was too much. The pain. The humiliation. The nausea that was beginning to edge in. The thoughts crashing through my brain, fighting for supremacy. The tear slid out of my eye, soaking into the lining of Snap's cut.

The next slid over the bridge of my nose on the same trajectory.

I felt something of him brush my shoulder.

His chest, I guessed, because then I felt his forehead pressed lightly against the side of my head and I heard his lips at my ear, that deep voice of his low and solemn, promising, "Got you now, baby. I got you. Nothing will ever hurt you again. Nothing, Rosie. Won't let it. Nothing, baby. Not a thing."

Another tear slid over the bridge of my nose.

And I heard the sirens.

* * * * *

Snapper

"Stand down, brother," Hop said at his ear.

Snapper had Speck up against the wall, their noses so close, the tips were brushing, Snap's hand around his throat, squeezing...*squeezing*. He had three brothers working him, trying to pull him off, but he had his weight aimed just right, straining against it, and he wasn't budging.

Speck stared into his eyes, not moving.

"Snap, man, everybody gets you," Rush said coaxingly. "Speck definitely gets you. Step off, man." Pause then, a jerk of his arm around Snap's chest, "*Step off*, brother."

"You were on her," Snapper clipped.

Speck just stared into his eyes, his face so red it was turning blue.

"You were supposed to look out for her," Snap carried on.

"He knows, Snap, look at him. Step *off*," Joker ordered.

Snapper kept squeezing.

Speck kept letting him.

"Brother, he fell down. He knows it. We'll deal with that later. We got two priorities here. Rosalie. And a reckoning for Bounty."

At Tack's voice, their leader, the president of the Chaos Motorcycle

Club, Snap pushed off of Speck, letting him go, and shrugged off Hop, Joker, and Rush's holds.

The second he felt them start to move away, he went back in, slamming his fist into the wall by Speck's head, feeling his knuckles split and Joker's arm coming around him to put him in a chokehold.

But Speck didn't even flinch.

Before he could try to make a move to plant his feet in order to throw Joke over his shoulder to get out of that hold, High had come in, caught Speck by the back of the neck and yanked him from the wall and away from Snapper's reach.

"Take your hands off me," Snapper bit at Joker.

Joker hesitated a second, felt Snap maneuvering his legs to break his hold, but when High had Speck well out of reach, he let go.

Joke stayed close, as did Hop and Rush, and Snapper's eyes didn't move from Speck.

"She was workin' that shit for us," he told Speck, and the whole room, something they knew. "We promised we had her back and you were on. You were supposed to *have her back*."

"He knows that. We all know that," Boz confirmed. "We're all feelin' this."

Snap turned on Boz. "Yeah? You got one guess who's feelin' it the most right now."

Boz winced.

"Yeah," Snap gritted. "And you didn't even see her, man. Beat to *shit*. She didn't have her waitress apron on and seein' her hair, I wouldn't have fuckin' recognized her."

"Fuck," Shy whispered.

Snapper slashed a glance through Shy but only allowed himself to do it at a slash.

Rosie had been Shy's once. He'd scraped her off, took up with Tab before he really even ended it with Rosalie. Cut her deep.

Sent her straight to Bounty.

To Throttle.

She hadn't wanted him at the hospital. She'd wanted him and Roscoe gone. But he'd heard. He'd heard that Throttle had delivered her ass to his brothers after he figured out Rosie was informing on Bounty's maneuvers with an enemy of Chaos.

She'd just wanted her man clean. Clean and clear of something that had two endings, one or the other certain: it'd either get him dead or incarcerated.

It seemed Rosie had bad taste in men.

That was going to change.

"Are we ridin' out on Bounty or what?" Hound snarled.

"They're fucked. Half of them are out on bail and Snap says first thing she asked for when she hit emergency was the police," Rush pointed out.

Hound took in Rush's words and then repeated to the room at large, "Are we ridin' out on Bounty or what?"

"We're riding out on Bounty."

That came quiet. Quiet and sinister.

From Tack.

Snapper moved first, yanking open the door to the Club's meeting room and running right into Tabitha Cage.

Shy's wife.

Tack's daughter.

"Is it true?" she snapped.

"Get outta the way, Tab," he said low.

Her eyes moved beyond him and she demanded, "Tell me it isn't true."

"Darlin', we're on this," her father said.

She took a step back and declared, "Yeah, we are. And I'm ridin' with Shy."

"Uh, say what?" Boz muttered from behind Snap.

"We don't have time for this shit," Snapper hissed.

"We actually don't, baby. We got work to do," Shy said.

"You're not in this either," Tack declared.

Shy pivoted on his father-in-law.

"Come again?" he asked.

"You're here," Tack decreed.

Were they seriously doing this?

Now?

Rosalie was still at the goddamned hospital. They were keeping her overnight.

He had asses to kick and a woman to get back to.

"Who's ridin' is ridin' and who isn't is stayin'," Snapper began and turned his head back to Tab, "and you are not riding."

"Says who?' she asked.

"Says me," he fired back.

"Excuse me but *she* is a sister who put her ass on the line for the Club and *I* am the sister who's gonna go kick their wuss asses in retribution. Ganging up for a beat down on a *girl*? Weak. Weak and lame," Tab returned.

"Don't you got a baby to look after?" Roscoe asked with more curiosity than refusal, and her narrowed eyes turned to him.

Then she lifted a hand, fingers clenched around a set of brass knuckles. Shy's brass knuckles. Hound got every brother a pair when they earned their patch. The palm grip had the Chaos emblem etched in and letters above each knuckle read one of the words from the Chaos motto: Wind, Fire, Ride or Free.

Shy's read "Wind."

Snapper's said "Ride."

"Don't you got a nose I can break?" she asked Roscoe back.

Snapper heard Hound's grim chuckle.

"Baby, give me my brass," Shy murmured.

"I'm riding!" she shouted.

"You're not and Shy's here but the rest of us are going," Tack declared.

"Dad!" she yelled.

"Tack," Shy clipped.

"Tabby, you wanna help, don't hold us up, we got shit to do," Tack growled then added, "And I'm thinkin' you get it's kinda important." He turned to Shy. "To do what we gotta do, you need control. You won't have control."

"Yeah, like Snap has control," Boz mumbled.

Snap felt his neck get tight, ready to take down a brother, even if that brother was Tack, to ride out on Bounty.

But Tack's eyes just slowly came to Snapper and he rumbled, "Snap is riding."

"Could that happen about now?" Snapper asked sarcastically.

"A statement has to be made by one of the Chaos women," Tab announced.

"Christ," Snapper hissed. "Can this stupid-ass shit be done?"

"Why is it stupid-ass?" Tab retorted. "'Cause I'm a girl?"

"Uh," he leaned toward her, "*yeah.*"

She leaned toward him. "That's what I call stupid-ass."

"We'll make your statement for you," Hound put in.

Tab turned her gaze on Hound and even Snapper lost track of what was happening and paid attention with the look that settled on her pretty face.

"You do not take your fists to a Chaos woman," she whispered. "You boys got an alarming trend goin' on with your women bein' caught up in your shit. So a Chaos woman needs to make a statement and Tyra might break a heel, Lanie might break a nail, Carissa probably doesn't even know how to form a fist, Millie already went through her trauma, Sheila's on the Western Slope, and Bev's at work, so this is on me and *I'm riding.*"

Tack was done.

So was Snap.

Tack got there before him.

"Deal with your woman," he ordered Shy. "Rosalie has reported the incident, we gotta get to them before the cops do. We don't have time for this. We need bail, you and Pete are on that." He finished with Shy and looked over his shoulder to his brothers. "The rest of you, let's ride."

"Dad!" Tab shouted, but Shy clamped an arm around her while the rest of the brothers rolled out.

They marched through the common room of the Compound to their bikes lined up at the front outside.

When they rode out, Tack was lead, Hop behind him with High riding next to Hop where Shy, as one of Tack's lieutenants (with Hop) and as the Club's Sergeant at Arms normally rode. But High made a motion to Hop and fell back. He then made a motion to Snap, who rode forward.

Of all of them, not that he'd left much in question bearing down on Speck like he had, High knew where his head was at with Rosalie.

It was a huge solid to take that place in formation.

It was late winter. Cold. Dark. Night had long fallen.

But Bounty would know they were coming.

They'd be prepared.

They'd be ready.

They'd be waiting.

And they were.

* * * *

Snapper sensed her waking up and looked over the top of his book to her.

He beat it back, the tight, hot feeling that welled up inside.

They'd laid Bounty out.

There was a lot of anger on both sides.

But Chaos had experience and skill. Joke used to be an underground fighter. Hound, Snap suspected, drank blood for breakfast and ate nails for dinner and outside that was all-around a lunatic. Boz was half-lunatic, but it was the good half when it came to a fight. High and Tack had had women they cared about messed up in bad shit, High recently, Tack not so much, but that shit never went away, so they were skilled as well at working out issues. Rush was all about the brotherhood and when the brotherhood had a mission, even if he didn't agree with it, he was always all in to carry out the mission. Hop had always been their hand-to-hand man. He used to play in a rock band but straight up, the way the man used his fists, he could have been a contender. Roscoe had seen Rosalie. Speck had making up to do.

And Snapper had incentive.

That incentive was right there, lying on the hospital pillow.

Her beautiful face was blown up, eyes swollen shut, lips inflamed, nose huge, broken, so taped. Red and mottled had given way to deep raisin-purple black, mostly around the eyes. There were livid scrapes and deep cuts that shared some of Bounty didn't bother taking off rings. There was flesh stitched together above and through her left eyebrow, along that side's jaw, and he knew, under the bandage at her nose, down the left side of the bridge.

Her throat was stippled with angry jam-colored bruising. Along the left side and at the top of her windpipe, there were distinct heavier discolorations where Throttle had dug the pads of his fingers in cruelly, positioned like he wanted to tear her throat out.

How Snap knew she was awake, he couldn't say. Her eyes were now so swollen they weren't open because she couldn't open them. But like earlier, he saw her long lashes fluttering so he clapped his book shut, set it aside, and leaned toward her.

"Hey," he whispered.

Her head had been turned to the side, his way.

She rolled it, facing the other way.

Snapper extended his fingers, flexing them before curling them in. They were swollen and mottled too, all the knuckles split and raw.

He didn't feel a thing.

He considered his next move.

He wasn't going to make her keep trying to escape him by rounding the bed.

Instead, he bent over her.

"You want some privacy, Rosie?" he asked.

She said nothing, just kept her battered face turned away.

"Baby, swelling will go down, bruises will recede and you'll be just as beauti—" he started to assure.

"Get out," she whispered.

Fuck.

Fuck!

"Rosie—"

"Get out," she repeated, still quiet, frail.

"We want an eye on you," he told her.

"No," she replied.

Snap leaned closer. "Honey—"

She turned her head so it was righted on her pillow and he saw just that pulled at and tightened her lips, showing him it caused pain.

They hadn't laid out Bounty enough.

Not near enough.

It was still feeble, but she kept at it. "No Chaos. No you. Get out."

"Rosie, we got them then the cops got them so you're safe, honey. But I wanna make sure you're safe so—"

"I never wanna see you again."

Snap froze.

"Get out," she reiterated.

"Rosie," he whispered.

"Everett, go."

She pulled out his real name.

This was more serious than the serious he already knew it was.

He tried again, mostly because he couldn't give up.

"Got up in Speck's shit, Rosie. Brothers are pissed. We rolled out on Bounty. All of us, we claimed you as one of our own. This didn't stand, Rosalie."

"I won't say it again," she whispered. "In five seconds I'm hitting the call button."

He put his hand over hers, which was actually at the call button.

She pulled it free, taking the button with her, and her mouth again got tight.

He didn't push that.

He tried another tack.

He shot her a grin. "C'mon, Scully. It's me. You know you got—"

It was the wrong thing to do.

"I'm not Scully and you are definitely not Mulder. We aren't out fighting for truth, having each other's backs."

Shit, that cut.

He leaned closer to her. "Baby, it's not on Speck. I know, the way it is between us, what we got...I fell down. I fell down lookin'—"

"It's done, Everett. It's over. I'm out. And you need to get gone."

Snap opened his mouth.

She lifted up the call button.

It was time to pull out the big shit.

"I'm in deep with you," he admitted softly.

"Then dig yourself out," she returned quietly, but her voice was harsh, ugly, and not just from having her throat squeezed to shit.

"I'll go now but I'll come back," he told her.

"Don't."

"I'm gonna take care of you."

"No you aren't."

"We're not done, you and me."

"Yes...we...*are*."

He got as close as he dared.

And he put it out there.

"I fell for you when you were Shy's and if you think that now, when you need me most, now, when I finally, fuckin' *finally* got a clear shot, I'm givin' up, think again, Rosie. You're hurt and you're pissed and I get that. But I'm not givin' you up. I don't care what way I gotta take you, as mine or just havin' you in my life in a way you'd let me be there, but however that is, I'm not givin' up. Not ever, Rosalie. I'm not givin' *you* up. You're gonna be in my life and I'm gonna be in yours. Bank on it."

He gave her that because he had to and she had to have it.

But he didn't push her further.

He reached up, kissed her forehead, straightened, grabbed his book…

And walked away.

For now.

Chapter One

Atone

Rosalie

I stood staring at myself in my mother's bathroom mirror.

I was going to have scars. Three of them.

Men with scars on their face were considered interesting, like they lived adventurous lives or were tough guys.

Women with them were looked on as pathetic, like some traumatic life event happened to them that they didn't survive without being marked and because of that were objects of sympathy.

Another discrepancy between the sexes which was absolutely not fair.

Like the difference in physical strength.

I was top heavy. Slender, long legs, slim hips, thin arms, but I had big boobs in a way they looked fake.

They weren't.

My mother had given me a number of good things, including her thick dark hair.

And her big tits.

My father had lamented this.

"Already hard enough to keep the men off you, gorgeous," he'd say to my mom. "And you got my ring on your finger and it's sat there for years. Now I got my baby girl to worry about."

Man.

I missed my dad.

I stopped thinking about my dad and stared at my torso in the mirror.

I'd learned over the span of my twenty-eight years of life that large breasts had awesome powers.

Helping you handle yourself when eight men were intent to beat the snot out of you was not part of those awesome powers.

I lifted my gaze and studied my face in the mirror.

They'd kept me in the hospital for two days, considering I'd taken a number of blows to the head, and thus had a serious concussion, and they tried to be cool about it, but I could tell they were concerned about the number of times I'd blacked out.

Now I'd been out of the hospital for two days, as, apparently (and thankfully) all systems were a go.

The swelling had decreased significantly but only that morning did I note that the bruising was starting to recede, some of the edges of the purple going yellow.

My broken nose was still taped and would be for some time.

I'd had a total of twenty-nine stitches sewn into my face. My eyebrow would never be the same. The jaw scar wouldn't be easily seen. But the gash on my nose would stand out.

I had been pretty, not beautiful, but definitely pretty. And I knew it.

This was not vanity. This was being real. I could see myself in the mirror and I'd had a mom and dad who adored me and told me how proud of me they were for a lot of reasons, and they'd done this all my life. My looks just were what they were and I was grateful for them.

I also used them.

I used them to get guys I was attracted to.

I used them to get good tips at Colombo's.

I used them to jump the line at clubs I wanted to get into.

And I used them to get out of that speeding ticket that time that cop pulled me over.

Mom had taught me, if God gave you something good, you didn't waste it. You used it (for good, obviously—I mean, it *was* God bestowing these gifts).

So I'd used them.

But as I stood there, looking in the mirror, I knew that Beck and his brothers had concentrated on my face, thinking that they were taking the most important thing I had away from me.

Men were so stinking stupid.

In the last few days, when there wasn't a lot to feel good about, I felt good about the fact that they hadn't raped me.

That was my silver lining.

My boyfriend kidnapped me, delivered me to his buds, they beat the heck out of me, but they didn't rape me.

If they'd done that to me, it would have taken away something that meant something.

But they hadn't.

Yeah.

Awesome silver lining.

Still, for sure it was one.

But, to my way of thinking, they didn't do any lasting damage. They didn't break anything but nine ribs (since I had twenty-four, that could have been worse) and my nose. When Muzzle's fist connected with my schnoz, I felt the cartilage give, and that hadn't been fun, but it would heal. Eightball had sprained my wrist, but he didn't snap it, and it had been tender but it was already feeling better.

I'd recover.

I could walk, talk, eat, breathe. I could definitely still deliver pizzas to diners' tables (or would be able to in a week or two, after the bruising and swelling were gone and I had less pain due to the broken ribs).

I might even be able to learn to live with the fact that a man I trusted and thought I loved had not only brought me to that hell, he'd also delivered his share of it.

Sure, I'd broken his trust. I'd informed on him and his brothers' activities to Chaos, setting them up to be taken down by the cops.

But let us not forget, they were able to be *set up to be taken down by the cops*. This meant they were doing felonious crap. That felonious crap being providing transport for illegal substances and firearms, offering this service to really bad guys.

So sure, I could see, if he found out, Beck being really freaking pissed at me. Yelling at me. Breaking it off with me. That was, if he didn't give me the chance to explain *why* I'd done it in the first place, that being for *him*.

Well, not so much for him, I'd realized.

But I couldn't think about that right then.

I had to think about the fact I survived. I was alive. Walking, talking, eating, breathing, and someday soon I'd again be laying pizza pies on tables for tips.

What I would not be doing was getting involved with a man, maybe ever again.

Seriously.

That might seem dramatic, but the first man I fell for, Shy Cage of the Chaos Motorcycle Club, had shown me a window to a world I wanted and the doorway I wanted to use to get to that was Shy because Shy was Shy. He was beautiful to look at and fantastic in bed, but he was also funny and sweet and protective and affectionate.

He was my dad (not that I knew about the "fantastic in bed" part with my dad, but from the time I understood the concept of sex, mom's dreamy looks and dad's cat-got-his-cream moods were not lost on me—gross, but not lost on me).

So Shy was all that...including having all of it on a bike.

But he dropped me like a hot brick the minute Tabitha Allen gave him indication that her doorway was open. He slammed the one on me and waltzed right through hers without a second thought.

Looking back, I knew as I fell deeper and deeper for him that he wasn't doing the same.

That didn't make it any better.

Now, also looking back, I knew as I got deeper and deeper into things with Beck that I was trying to find what I'd hoped to get with Shy.

They both belonged to motorcycle clubs, for one.

And Beck looked a lot like Shy for another (which, not so by the by, was a lot like my dad looked). Beefier, maybe. A bit rougher around the edges. But I definitely had a type.

And then came Snapper.

God, Snapper.

Nope.

No.

No more men for me.

Seriously.

Shy.

Then Beck? (Enough said there.)

And then there was Snap.

I closed my eyes and shook my head just as I heard a knock on the bathroom door.

"Sweetie," Mom called through the door. "You been in there a long time. You okay?"

She was worried about me.

She would be. She was a mom. An awesome one. And when your daughter gets hospitalized due to her boyfriend and his motorcycle club stomping the crap out of her, that was definitely something that made moms worry.

But she'd been worried before that. She was part of the reason I'd made the deal with Chaos in the first place.

My dad had been a biker. He was a nomad when it came to that kind of thing (or, really, any kind of thing). He accepted being tied down by his woman and his daughter only, not anything else. Not a job. Not a mortgage. Not a membership to a club. He hung with a lot of them, including Chaos (in fact, Hammer, sadly now deceased, but one of the founding members of Chaos, had been my father's best friend).

But he'd never hung with Bounty.

"Don't like the feel of them," I'd heard him mutter years ago. "If you're an outlaw, own the outlaw. If you're not, own that. You can't wanna be a Gypsy Joker. You either are or you aren't. They wanna be. But they aren't. That shit just ain't right and it could get dangerous."

He'd been right.

It got dangerous.

I should have known.

I should have followed my dad.

Mom and me had done it all our lives, job to job, house to house, city to city.

Why I stopped…

Damn.

I knew why I'd stopped.

I'd wanted Shy, Shy, who reminded me of Dad.

And when I couldn't have him, I'd gone looking.

I'd wanted what my mom had.

I'd wanted that sweetness. That love.

That devotion.

I'd wanted the stability that just seeped down deep into your bones from all that no matter the job changing, the scenery changing, the amount of times you boxed up a house.

Stability had nothing to do with income and locale.

Stability was all in the heart.

"Rosalie, honeypot, you okay?" Mom called.

"Yeah," I called back. "Out in a sec."

"There are some…uh, people here for you," she told me.

I focused on my battered face in the mirror.

People?

"Who?" I asked.

"Well, uh…"

I didn't like that she didn't answer immediately.

I went to the door and opened it.

And there I was, standing before me, just a little older.

Dark hair, but she was letting the thick silver settle in. It looked gorgeous on her.

Hazel eyes that could change to more green or more light brown depending on what color she (or I) wore.

Tall*ish*. We were both five six. We seemed taller because our length was in our legs and we were slender.

We also tanned easily. Laughed easily. But were mostly quiet, sometimes shy but not withdrawn, just not loud and feisty.

"Christ, God loves me," my dad had said. "Gave me the perfect woman and then gave me her carbon copy so I get double the goodness."

I remembered him saying that. We were living outside San Francisco then in a little two-bedroom house where we could smell the sea and Mom had a big garden. I remembered how happy he was.

Always happy.

Always right where he wanted to be.

With his girls, his bike close, the world at his feet…or in Dad's case, his wheels.

I remembered those words he'd said nearly every time I looked at my mom.

And I hoped I never forgot.

"Who's here?" I asked.

"Kane Allen and his old lady," she said softly.

Damn.

"And also, um, his lieutenant and *his* old lady," she went on.

Damn!

Shy was his lieutenant.

I'd run into Shy and Tabby in a mall not long after he'd dumped me. I was now over him and not just because I had no choice since he was not only married to Tab, they also had a baby, but because I just was.

And now I was even more because I'd figured out I wasn't over Shy because I'd had Beck.

But because I'd wanted Snapper.

"I don't want to see them," I told my mom.

"It's Hopper Kincaid, not the other one," she replied quickly.

Well, at least Shy and Tabby didn't march their way to my mother's house to do whatever Kane "Tack" Allen and Hop Kincaid were there to do, this after the guy who came next when Shy was done with me got *done with me*.

"I still don't want to see them," I said.

"Honey, they…" She looked down the hall then back to me. "I don't think it's a good idea to refuse an audience with Kane Allen."

She was right.

The Chaos Club had left their outlaw ways behind and was now clean, but that didn't mean the brothers were men you trifled with. And of all of them, you didn't trifle with Kane Allen.

It wasn't just in the physical (though he was physically intimidating). It was that the man was known to be killer smart. If he perceived a slight and wanted to act on it, that could come in so many different ways, none of them pleasant, it wasn't funny.

"Right," I muttered to Mom, then, being careful with my body because other parts might be healing, but my ribs still hurt like hell, I rounded her and walked stiffly down the hall, feeling her at my heels.

And there they were. Two fabulously handsome brothers of Chaos—Tack Allen and Hop Kincaid. They were older, sure, but they were still crazy-hot.

They were also, right then, the instant their eyes touched on me, crazy-freaky-*scary*.

It was not unknown in the Denver biker world that Chaos took the mistreatment of women seriously, as in, they seriously one hundred percent did not like it (one of the reasons why I used to hang at their Compound a lot, where I'd met Shy).

Now I was getting a dose of that in my mom's living room.

As the keeper of a vagina, I had to admit, it was cool.

That didn't make it less crazy-freaky-scary.

To avoid the crazy-freaky-scary, I looked to the women with them.

Tack had had Tyra when I was with Shy. She was gorgeous, curvy, and had deep-red, beautiful hair.

The tall, slim, beautiful brunette with Hop was familiar, but for Hop, as far as I knew, she was new.

"Hey," I greeted.

"How you doin', darlin'?" Tack asked.

"Healing. Good. Thanks for checking but it wasn't necessary. Every day it gets better and soon I'll be back to new," I answered.

Or new with scars, so a new kind of new.

"That's good," he muttered, staring intently at me.

"So, well…" I hesitated because I didn't want to say what I said next but I'd grown up around clubs, I knew the drill, and respect needed to be shown. "Do you all want something to drink or something?"

"We're here to share that we've got your place sorted out," Tyra spoke up.

"I…" That threw me. "Sorry?"

"Throttle's still in the hospital," Hop's deep voice sounded and I looked to him. "He's being released today into police custody."

I'd heard about my ex-man, this coming from the police who were keeping me informed about my situation. Thus I knew, before the cops got to him, someone had carved into his face with a blade.

My guess, Hound. I'd heard rumors when he went to work he didn't mess around.

I had mixed feelings about this.

As a human being, I did not condone slicing someone's face with a knife.

As the woman who'd been strangled and beaten by her boyfriend only to be turned over to all his friends to have a go, it didn't bother me all that much.

"Doesn't matter," Hop went on. "We figure you wouldn't want to go back there so the boys went and got your shit, moved it into a new pad. It's Chaos. We've had it secured. The women have sorted your things. So you're good to move in whenever you're healed up."

As he finished, Tack walked to me, lifting his hand.

Dumbly, I lifted mine too and he dropped a key ring in it with a number of keys on it.

I stared at the keys in my palm as my mom asked, "How is it secured?"

"Security system," Tack answered. "Doors, windows, garage. Direct dispatch callout if breached. When you go in, the garage door openers are on the kitchen counter."

I looked to him then I turned to my mother.

The relief was practically glowing a golden aura around her body.

Damn.

"The system is top of the line and those Bounty boys broke their bond agreements so they won't be let out prior to their hearing, and now most of them will be standing trial for more than just the runs they were making," Tack continued. I looked back to him to see his attention directed at Mom. "Still, we're not takin' any chances," his eyes came to me, "so we'll continue to have a brother on you."

Okay.

That wasn't happening.

"That isn't necessary," I murmured.

"We'll agree to disagree on that," he returned firmly.

That meant: You're moving into the space we're offering you and accepting our protection and there will be no discussion on either.

I, however, was feeling a discussion was necessary.

"Mr. Allen—" I started.

"I'm Tack to you, darlin'," he cut me off, now speaking gently. "Always have been, nothin's changed that."

I stared him right in the eye.

"Mr. Allen," I repeated resolutely, watched his jewel-blue eyes flash and his mouth set tight but I didn't care, and this time he didn't interrupt me. "I'm sure you can imagine that I'm keen to move on from all that's happened and I appreciate your concern. But if you'll tell me where you took my stuff, Mom and I'll go get it. I'm not Chaos's problem anymore."

"'Fraid at this point that's not something that's ever gonna change," he replied. "Not that you're a problem, sweetheart. Just that you're ours and we take care of our own."

That felt good but I couldn't let it feel good.

So I didn't.

"I appreciate your loyalty but what I'm trying to communicate is that I'm out."

"Rosalie," Hop said in a quiet tone, "you know, honey, once you're in there's never an out."

I'd hoped for that…once.

I'd hoped to be a part of their family and never let go.

But I didn't get it.

And now I didn't want it.

(Okay, so I was just telling myself that but I hoped to get in that mindset in, say, five days to fifteen years.)

"I've never been in," I returned.

"Sweetheart." It was now Tack who was giving me the quiet. "You're Chaos and you know it. You know how you are. But I'm guessin' you know how deep that goes now, am I right?"

"Because I put my neck out for you and nearly got it wrung?" I asked, watching some of the crazy-freaky-scary come back at a reminder of what happened to me.

"There's that and there's more, and I 'spect if you don't know what that more is now, it won't be long before you find out," he answered.

That was *definitely* not going to happen.

I opened my mouth to share that when Tyra stepped forward.

"Kane, why don't you and Hop step outside?" she suggested.

He turned his head toward his woman. "We're not steppin' outside."

"Okay then." She gave in immediately, but didn't give up. "How about you back off?"

"Red—" he began.

"Tack, let me," she whispered.

He studied her.

Then he backed off.

She came closer to me and the brunette approached with her.

Mom got closer to my side.

When she did, that was when I wanted to cry.

We'd lost Dad three years ago and I, honest to God, to that day, did not know how either of us had survived it.

But I knew there'd come a time, and I prayed it would be far in the future, when I'd face a world without my mother in it and I didn't know how I'd manage it.

"Hey, Rosalie," Tyra greeted like she'd just walked in.

"Tyra," I replied.

She tipped her head toward the brunette. "You remember Lanie?"

Right, yes, I remembered then. Her name was Lanie and she was Tyra's best friend, now Hop's old lady.

I checked out the other woman and noted again she was incredibly beautiful and had my body structure, with more length and less breast tissue.

"Yeah, I saw you around the Compound," I said, then gave her a "Hey."

"Hi, Rosalie," she responded on a small smile. "Nice to officially meet you."

I nodded and gestured to my side. "Did you guys meet my mom?"

"Yes," Tyra answered. "We introduced ourselves when we came in."

"Great," I said, not meaning it, and that sounded in the word.

"I think I need to explain something to you," she declared.

"I'm not sure you do," I retorted.

Mom got closer and linked her pinkie with mine.

I held on tight.

Tyra kept talking like I hadn't.

"They're feeling this."

Damn it.

Now I was getting mad.

"They are?" I asked sarcastically.

"They made you a promise and they didn't keep it," she pointed out.

"I made my own decisions and I knew the consequences," I returned.

She kept on her bent.

"They are not men who don't keep promises."

I shut up in order to let her finish so this could be done.

"They need to keep that promise now, Rosalie. They need to look out for you," she shared.

"And what if I don't want them to look out for me?" I asked.

She gave me an amused smile, a short shake of her head, and

replied, "That doesn't factor."

I stared at her. "That's crazy."

She then gave a slight shrug. "That's Chaos."

Okay, I was fed up with this.

"Listen, the police are involved," I informed her, though I knew she knew. "I'm done with Throttle. Throttle is *way* done with me. They meted out their brand of justice. I contacted the authorities to mete out mine. I don't know if there's anything more to play out but that doesn't matter for you guys. Chaos has no part in this anymore. When Throttle took me to his brothers, it became about him and them and me."

"There is no you," Tyra told me.

That ticked me off.

"Of course there's a me," I snapped.

"Not when you belong to Chaos," she volleyed.

I heard Mom take in a breath.

"I don't belong to Chaos," I returned.

"Honey," she said softly, "even if the brothers, each and every one of them, didn't claim you because of what you did for the Club and what you endured because they fell down in protecting you, which they do, you're Snap's."

Oh no.

Not on your life.

I started to say something but she lifted her hand and kept going.

"I'm so sorry. This is a lot. So much is happening to you, Rosalie, and I hate that for you. But you can lie to me. You can lie all you want. Just never lie to yourself. You know where that stands better than I do. A brother claims a woman, she's owned by the Club, and when it's Chaos, that's a good thing. Trust me."

"I am currently, and for the foreseeable future, not property of any member of the male species," I declared, then, for good measure, decided to add, "Especially not a biker."

"I'll leave that part up to Snap," she muttered.

"Okay, Tyra, listen—" I started angrily.

"Rosalie," she whispered. "Please, I'm begging you, let us take care of you. We *need* to take care of you."

At the sincerity in her tone and the look in her eyes that shared she knew my pain in a lot of ways right then, I went still.

And when I went still, my mom's pinkie released mine so she could curl all her fingers around all of mine.

"I can understand that right now, you don't want us, but for us, you're our family and you're feeling pain and in a serious situation that was caused by our issues," Tyra explained. "Think about that. Think about how you'd feel if the role was reversed, if you were me standing in front of a woman who had what happened to you happen to her. How would you feel? What would you need to do?"

"And how, precisely," I began acidly, "did what happened to me become about you?"

"Because we need to atone and you're you and you're the kind of person with the kind of heart who'll need to allow us to do it."

Damn it!

I was.

I was that person.

That person Dad taught me to be.

That person Mom taught me to be.

Not to mention I hated it they were feeling this so deeply. They didn't beat the crap out of me and they couldn't provide 24/7 protection, I knew that from the beginning. I mean, I was living with Beck, for goodness sakes.

I also hated being snarky.

So I clamped my mouth shut.

Mom giggled just a little.

I turned a glare toward her and saw instantly she wanted Chaos to take care of me really, *really* badly.

Damn it!

Lanie took a step forward, digging in the slick clutch she'd had tucked under her arm, a slick clutch that went with her slick outfit of tailored trousers, fabulous feminine blouse, and magnificent heels that did not say "Biker Old Lady" but instead said, "Givenchy Thinks This Chick Is The Shit."

She pulled out a piece of paper and handed it to me.

It was thick, almost like cardstock, and had a cool logo of an advertising agency on the top with the name *Elaine Kincaid, CEO* under it with something written below.

I'd missed that news.

She wasn't just Hop's old lady, they'd gotten hitched.

"That's the address for your new place. It's close to Colombo's and close to your mom. Actually, a lot closer than your old place," she said.

I stared down at the address and saw she told no lies. It was probably a ten-minute ride from Mom's place and the same from Colombo's.

Last, it was the same from Ride, the auto supply store and custom car and bike garage that Chaos owned where their Compound was also located.

In other words, it was smack in what certain citizens of Denver knew with zero doubts was Chaos territory, owned, controlled, and patrolled by the brothers.

I'd lived in Aurora, a suburb southeast of Denver, with Beck.

In terms of club turf, that address was like I was moving to a different country.

Well, at least I could shave off forty minutes from my work commute.

"My number is also on that, as is Tyra's," Lanie shared. "If you like, we'd love to show you and Renae," she gestured with a hand to Mom, "your new space." She gave me a grin. "It's really cute."

"And who do I pay rent to?" I asked pointedly.

Tack rejoined the conversation by growling, "That's covered."

"Kane," Tyra said under her breath.

Okay, this I couldn't give in on. I paid my own way.

"Absolutely unacceptable," I said on top of mine.

"For a few months," Lanie cut in. "Just a few months. After you settle in, get healed up, we'll talk about rent."

"How do I know it'll be something I can afford?" I asked.

"It'll be something you can afford," Hop answered.

"Hop," Lanie said sharply.

"We'll hammer all that out when the time comes," Tyra put in.

"This is wonderful, thank you," Mom said.

And that, as was Mom's way, was that.

My voice was a lot like hers (in times not like this one, but Mom's never wavered), delicate and melodious. Soothing. Peaceful. I could probably count on one hand how often she'd raised her voice that I remembered. Even in heavy situations, when folks were upset or angry, if Mom waded in, her calm, the tranquility of her voice, assured and settled pretty much any situation.

And right then it said she appreciated what they were doing for her daughter, but she and I were both done with this conversation.

I'd had years of Mom being able to pull that kind of thing off.

I was still surprised to see it work on Tack Allen and Hopper Kincaid.

"Appreciate you ladies givin' us time," Tack murmured. "And good to see you're healin', sweetheart," he said to me.

"We'll just head out," Hop added, making a move with Tack.

"Call us when you go to your new place," Lanie urged. "Or…you have the keys, if you go, give us a bell and tell us what you think."

"Right, thanks," I replied.

"And if you need anything…" Tyra let that trail.

I just nodded to her and gave her a tight smile.

"Thank you for coming," Mom said, making her own move to the door.

I stayed where I stood.

"See you later," Lanie said to me.

"Mm-hmm," I hummed noncommittally.

"'Bye, Rosalie," Tyra said.

I nodded to her again.

Tack and Hop gave me looks and jerked up their chins.

A week ago I would have found that hot.

Now I thought…

Men.

Mom murmured good-byes and thank yous and see you laters and I stood watching her as she ushered them out and closed the door on them.

Only when the door was closed did I walk through the room to the front window.

I looked out, intent to watch them drive away.

But what I saw made me suck in breath.

Snap was out there.

Now talking in a close-huddle, heads-bent way with Tack and Hop while Lanie and Tyra drifted toward the truck and SUV in our driveway, Snap's bike at the curb.

He was out there.

Shy was tall, dark and lanky.

Beck was tall, dark and stocky.

Snap was blond, shorter than both Shy and Beck, (taller than me), with an athletic build that was both powerful and lean. He had thick eyebrows darker than his hair and a blond beard that was dark under his jaws, light everywhere else, clipped short and groomed, mostly, but long at the chin.

His hair came down to his shoulders and he almost always wore it in a messy bun at the back, but if he kept it down, he slicked it back with something so it stayed out of his face.

He had amazing cheekbones, a beautiful lower lip, and gorgeous, strong white teeth that shone bright against skin that was always tan due to his ride being a bike.

All that was fantastic.

But for me with Snap it was the eyes.

His eyes reminded me of a husky dog's eyes. If you looked closely enough (and until recently I hadn't allowed myself to pay attention to the fact that I did…a lot), they weren't the light blue that they seemed to be at a glance.

Most of the iris was almost like snow and the blue cast they had came from a rim of sky at the edge of the iris and the edge of the pupil, both that bled into the white.

I'd never seen eyes like Snapper's.

You would think that snow would put you in a deep freeze but he'd never, not once, not even for an instant, given me anything cold.

He was all warm for me.

It was a hair down day for Everett "Snapper" Kavanaugh, slicked back, whatever he used making the light blond seem darker.

It was also an intent day, I could tell by the serious look on his face while he was listening to Tack speak.

He wasn't going to invade my space because I'd kicked him out of my hospital room (God, that was *so* Snapper).

But he wasn't waiting even for a phone call to learn how I was. He was getting a briefing on me. Everything. From how I looked to how I held myself to how I behaved to how I reacted to what they'd offered me (or, more accurately, what I'd been forced to accept).

You're gonna be in my life and I'm gonna be in yours. Bank on it.

"Is that him?" Mom whispered from beside me, standing so close our arms brushed.

She knew everything. Everything about everything. Around the time I turned seventeen, she started the long process of morphing from

just my mom, to my mom and sometimes friend, to my friend and
sometimes mom, to my best friend who was also the precious being
who had birthed me.

"That's him," I whispered back.

He nodded and I knew by the movements of his body he was going
to disconnect, so I quickly moved out of the window, doing it watching
and seeing his head turning my way.

Standing out of sight, thus losing sight of Snapper before he caught
sight of me, I watched my mother wave at him.

"Mom!" I hissed.

"He's really cute," she said.

He was. He was really cute in a hot-guy, badass biker kind of way.
Take off the leather cut, trim his hair, shave his beard, and he'd be the
boy next door.

The boy next door you were itching to get in your bed and would
sell your soul to earn the honor of having his ring on your finger.

To escape what was happening at the window, I turned so my
shoulders were against the wall and looked down at the paper in my
hand.

Elaine Kincaid, CEO of an advertising agency.

Hop had married a business lady.

Surprising and interesting.

And cool.

I stared at the address under it, focusing on it rather than the fact
that Snap was right outside.

Suddenly, my eyes narrowed on it.

As they did, I recollected a conversation I'd had with Snap, one of
many I shouldn't have had when he was just supposed to be my contact
with Chaos, sharing with him what I'd heard Beck say his brothers were
up to when it came to antisocial activities, not to mention I was living
with another guy.

How many properties? I'd asked, aghast at the intel about himself
he'd shared over the course of our by then hour-long phone
conversation.

*Five, no…six. But, babe, it isn't a big deal. All the brothers get a cut
of Ride and both the store and garage do a huge turnover. It is what it is
but the way I live my life, what am I gonna do with that kind of money?*
he'd answered.

I could think of a lot of things to do with that kind of money, I'd told him.

Yeah, well, I'm not big on shoes, he'd replied. *So I buy houses.*

I'd laughed.

I had to admit, I liked shoes.

What I didn't admit was that I liked that Snapper had noticed.

He'd listened to me laughing for a while before he'd said, *I can't just sit on it. I got it, gotta make it work for me.*

So I guess you buy six properties and let it work, I'd teased.

Yeah, he'd said with a smile in his voice. *Comes time, I'll be good. My woman will be good. Our kids wanna go to some expensive college, they'll be good. They want big weddings, that'll be good. We wanna take crazy huge family vacations, that'll be good. Or if a shit storm hits, we'll be covered.*

I didn't remember my reply to that, just that I'd turned the topic of conversation.

But I remembered how what he'd said made me feel.

I stared at the address on the paper.

Tack had said the place they'd put me in was Chaos.

But I knew it wasn't just Chaos, as such.

It was Snapper.

He had six rental properties, a couple were condos, the rest small homes.

This was his.

He was giving this to me.

He probably had someone evicted so he could give it to me.

I drew in breath as I heard a motorcycle roar to life.

"Rosalie?" Mom called.

I shifted just enough I could see out the window and watched Hop pull out with Lanie at his side in his truck. Tack and Tyra in their huge SUV were already out and driving away.

I shifted more and saw the curb was empty but I knew that already, the sound of Snap's pipes were fading.

"Honey," Mom murmured and I looked to her. "You okay?"

"This," I waved the note in the air, "is Snap's."

"Sorry?" she asked.

"This place they moved me into without my permission or agreement or even really acceptance. Snapper owns it."

"Oh," she murmured, her eyes drifting reverently to the paper.

Yep.

Reverently.

She'd always liked Chaos too. She used to party with them with Dad back in the day before I came along.

The thing I was worried about was that she'd start to get to like Snapper, especially before she'd even met him.

This could happen. He was just that likable. An all-around good guy. Easy on the eyes. Easy to talk to. Easy to be with. Sweet, smart, thoughtful.

It was my turn to call her attention to me.

"Mom."

She looked right into my eyes.

"Please, Rosalie, let them take care of you."

I closed my eyes.

I opened them.

"You did the right thing with Beck and his club," she said when I did. "I'm proud of you. Your father would have been proud of you, though he wouldn't have let you do it."

That made my lips quirk.

Then again, Dad would have been on me about being with Beck at all. He'd let me make my own decisions, but that didn't mean he wouldn't have something to say about it.

"He still would have been glad you considered it," she carried on. "It went bad. He's not here to keep you safe and I—"

"Mom—"

"But they can," she finished determinedly. "I'm here to listen, you want to talk. I'm here to hold on to, you want to let it out. I'm here to get angry right along with you, you want to rail and scream. Whatever you need from me, I'm here. But I can't give you that. I can't keep you safe. *You* can't keep you safe. But they can and…" she swallowed then pushed it out, "Bounty is not done with you."

I drew breath in through my nose, ticked my mom was worried, ticked at Beck, ticked at myself, but she was and there was nothing I could do about it so I nodded.

"We'll go look at it soon, okay?" I offered.

"We should ask Tyra and Lanie to meet us," she suggested.

I shook my head. "I don't think getting deeper into that crew is a good idea."

To that she stated, "He's handsome."

She was talking about Snap.

"Yeah, he is, but—"

"He's yours."

I shut my mouth.

Mom didn't.

"Standing outside in the cold, waiting for word about you, putting you in his place so he knows you're safe, he's yours like Beck never was, like that other one never was. He's yours. He's yours to break or he's yours to hold safe."

"Chaos men are unbreakable," I informed her.

"If your father lived to see his daughter in that hospital bed like I saw her, he'd have shattered," she retorted.

And that's when the tears started to sting my eyes.

"Men are breakable, Rosalie," she said in her calm, serene voice. "They just hide the cracks better than we women do."

"I thought he was going to kill me," I whispered.

She stood solid and held my gaze, hers suddenly bright like mine was, filled with wet, knowing I was now talking about Beck.

"He'd kissed that neck he'd nearly squeezed the life from so many times, I couldn't count them," I told her.

My mom stood there and kept hold of me, warm and safe, using nothing but her gaze.

"Do you think I want to jump into another situation with another biker?" I asked.

"Your father was a biker," she reminded me.

"My father was one of a kind," I reminded her.

"He died and you went searching," she stated.

This, I couldn't handle. I knew it. I understood it. I was coming to terms with the mistakes I'd made.

But hearing it come from my mother's lips, I couldn't deal with it.

So I looked out the window at our dead winter lawn, our empty driveway, the curb bare.

"You found that Chaos boy, the first one, as a replacement," she said, careful, gentle, sweet.

I swallowed.

She was right.

Dad had died.

I'd been lost.

Then I found Shy.

"He wouldn't keep you, you went reeling," she kept on.

I saw nothing but clear, hot waves rippling before my eyes.

"Then you latched on to the next thing that reminded you of what you lost," she said.

I'd done that for sure.

My voice was trembling when I replied, "I messed up."

"You were grieving."

I turned to her, shaking my head fiercely to shake the tears from my eyes, and repeated, "I messed up."

"Okay, that wasn't what I was trying to get through to you, I was simply trying to guide your way to understanding the path you've been on. But if you have to look at it that way, sure, okay, you messed up," she agreed half-heartedly. "Though it burns me that any woman takes responsibility for the callous brutality a man can inflict, that burn runs deeper I hear that come from my own daughter's mouth, but for now, I'll let that be and just say, my beautiful girl, don't mess up again."

"Life is not about finding a man," I told her.

"Life is about finding happy," she told me. "So don't," she jerked her head to the window, "*mess up.*"

"They all went at me, Mom." Now I was talking about Bounty.

She'd pulled it together.

With that, it killed, but the water hit her eyes and she couldn't contain it.

It started leaking down her cheeks.

"I'm sorry," I whispered. "I shouldn't lay that on you. Not you."

"Rosalie, honeypot," she began, lifting her hands to brush away the tears, "pray to God you learn, and when you do, trust me, you'll learn that as difficult as it is to take, as heavy as any burden might be, when a woman becomes a mother, she can bear anything for her child. So lay it on me."

"I'm scared," I told her.

"Of course," she told me.

"I can't think of another guy right now," I shared.

"That's understandable," she replied.

"I just have to get through today."

"Then we'll get you through it."

"I loved him before," I whispered the admission. "Before what happened happened to me."

"What?" she whispered back.

"I wanted to make Beck into Snap."

"Oh, Rosie," she breathed, finally coming toward me, and if I wasn't wrong, there was a grin playing at her lips.

"Mom, it was stupid," I said as she lifted both hands and held my jaw carefully.

She tipped her head toward me, eye to identical eye.

"I just need to get through today," I restated.

"How can I help with that?" she asked.

"Do you have Tillamook salted butterscotch ice cream?"

"Is my little girl in the vicinity?"

My grin was shaky and my nod in her hands was jerky.

"Spoons and the container and a marathon of Jason Bourne?" she proposed.

My grin got less shaky and my nod was far more definite.

"You're on TV duty, I'll get the ice cream," she decreed.

She then came in, brushing her cheek against mine before she let me go and moved toward the kitchen.

"Mom?" I called.

She turned to me.

"I'm sorry you have to go through this with me," I said.

"Something else you'll learn, I pray, my beauty, is the good, the bad, the ugly, a mother is never sorry. Their baby needs them, there's no other place they would be."

Yes, oh yes.

I'd never manage without her.

"I love you," I told her.

"And there it is," she replied simply.

Then she went to get the ice cream.

I watched her go, knowing she was right.

There it was.

That was us. Our family. Our life.

We'd never had a mortgage (Mom still rented). We'd never had roots.

But we'd had each other.

And love.

And that was all that was needed.

So life sucked right then, it was uncertain and scary, both of those things in the extreme.

But I had my mom.

And that was all that was needed.

On that thought, I moved to the TV.

Chapter Two

Path

Rosalie

A plethora of guns lay in display cabinets before me, lined up on their sides, white tags attached to them.

A little old man with not a lot of hair (in fact, there were about three strands wafting over his shiny dome) was on the opposite side of the case, just down, eyeing me as I assessed my options.

I could imagine what I looked like. What with it being just a couple days after Tack, Hop, Tyra, and Lanie came to call, I was still bruised and stitched up with a taped nose, angry welts across my neck, and moving gingerly.

He probably thought I was a woman with revenge on my mind.

I wasn't.

I was a woman with protection on my mind.

Chaos said they were going to cover me but they'd said that before and no protection was infallible (as I'd learned the hard way).

This time, I wasn't going to take any chances.

The little old guy didn't approach me, which I thought was weird. He worked there and I was a customer. I had questions. I mean, I could pick a gun that fit in any one of my purses (or at least most of my purses—I was equal opportunity with purses, and wallets, seeing as if the purse was smaller, the wallet would also have to be) but I also needed one I could handle.

Further, I needed to learn how to handle it.

According to the Yelp listing, Zip's Gun Emporium was the place for all your gun and ammo needs, offering admittedly crotchety (and there were a fair few reviews that shared this information), but nevertheless expert gun and ammo advice.

The listing also shared it had a firing range.

And whoever Zip was, he taught classes.

He did it grumpily, but he was reportedly good at it.

But there weren't any notices up anywhere about these classes. The only things on the walls were shotguns, rifles, and more handguns, as well as the odd mostly-naked-chick poster mingled with mostly-naked-chick calendars.

I needed a gun and to sign up for a class.

So I needed to talk to somebody.

"You takin' this?" I heard asked.

I looked in the direction this came from, which was toward the old guy, who I saw was not speaking to me, just as I heard, "Yup."

That was when I turned even further, which was right before I froze.

Snapper was moving toward me.

He was doing it also doing a full body scan, up, down, back up again, down, then back up, gaze lingering on my throat, then on my face, and finally he made it to me, stopped and looked into my eyes.

It was a man-bun day as well as about six days past grooming his beard.

And I knew it was six days because I felt it hit my lower belly that those six days since I was hurt were six days he spent worrying about me and not bothering with what he considered was unnecessary personal grooming.

"Hey," his baritone came at me.

"Hey," I said quietly.

"How you doin'?" he asked.

"Good," I answered.

His teeth came out and hit dead center in his full lower lip in a way I instantly became mesmerized.

They let that lip go to whisper, "Rosie."

I lifted my gaze to his.

"What you doin' in a gun shop, honey?" he asked.

I thought that was a stupid question and was surprised by it because Snap was not a stupid guy.

"I think that's kinda obvious," I pointed out since he was looking right at me and the swelling might be gone but the rest was still visible.

"How 'bout we go get some coffee," he suggested.

I shook my head. "I need to buy a gun today so I can get started on the waiting period thingie."

His mouth moved in a way I'd never seen before and he didn't respond immediately. I would understand why when he did and it was tentative.

"Colorado doesn't have a waiting period."

He didn't want me to know that.

He didn't want me owning a gun.

He still told me that.

So Snapper.

"Snapper—" I began.

He got closer.

I shut up because, first, he got closer, and second, because when he did, I could smell him, leather and soap and outdoors and all of that together on Snapper smelled beautiful, and last, once he got closer, he just *was* closer.

"Come have coffee with me," he urged.

"I need a gun," I whispered.

"You don't need a gun, Rosie."

"I need a gun, Snapper."

"You don't know how to handle a gun," he pointed out.

"I'm gonna take lessons," I shared.

He looked in my eyes then said, "Zip," without breaking my gaze.

The little old man showed across the case at our sides.

"You got the binder?" Snapper asked, again not looking away from me.

"Boy, you're gonna blow a sale for me," the little old guy, apparently the Zip of Zip's Gun Emporium, said by way of answer.

That was when Snapper turned his head, just his head, his body didn't move from facing me.

"Chaos buy exclusive from Zip's?" he asked.

"You came by coupla days ago, warned me about her," Zip said and that was when I looked to him just in time to catch him jerking his bald head my way. "I heard you and agreed to give you the heads up, she showed. Now I *see* her, and if she wants it, I'm sellin' this girlie a gun."

Okay, I couldn't handle the explanation of why Snapper was there and that was the fact that it was apparent he'd made the rounds of gun shops in order to stop me from doing something he thought might be foolhardy.

And since I couldn't handle that, I had to focus on something else.

"Thank you," I said to Zip.

"I can impose my own waiting period and I'm doin' that," Zip said to me. "You can't have a gun until your ass is in my range and I'm feelin' good you can handle yourself with it."

"Works for me," I replied.

"Rosie," Snapper said low.

I looked to him. "I'm getting a gun, Snap."

He turned again to Zip.

"You wanna lose Chaos business?" he threatened.

Zip didn't blink. "What I want is a world where this shit," he jabbed a finger my way, "doesn't walk in my doors. That miracle happens, I'll close those doors. That miracle ain't gonna happen. So you boys take your business elsewhere," he shrugged, "that'd suck balls. But this girlie feels safer with a firearm in her purse, I'll get over it."

Sadly, I wasn't the first beat-to-hell woman who'd walked through his doors looking for protection.

Or a means to get revenge.

Surprisingly, Zip was the kind of man who cared about it.

"That's sweet," I noted.

"Shee-it," he muttered. "I ain't sweet."

"But it was sweet, what you just said," I disagreed.

"See," he started, "I wanna arm you so whatever motherfucker did that shit to your face...and your throat...you got the means to drill holes in him. That ain't sweet."

Okay, maybe it wasn't sweet.

"It was eight mothereffers who did this," I shared.

His eyes got big.

Then they got mad.

Then they got mean.

After that, they snapped to Snapper.

"This the girl Bounty worked over?" he asked.

"You heard," Snap remarked.

"All over the street," Zip declared. "Always been useless assholes. Now I'm more glad you Chaos boys carved those dipshits up."

"She's got Chaos protection," Snapper stated.

"Yeah, I get that, you're here," Zip returned.

"So she doesn't need a gun," Snapper concluded.

"She yours?" Zip asked.

"Yes," Snapper said.

"No," I said at the same time.

Zip looked between Snap and me, an expression of resignation slid over his features, and he mumbled, "Christ, not another one of these."

I didn't know what that meant but I quickly carried on in hopes of ensuring a sale for ole Zip, "I have a mom. We're close. She could become a Bounty target if they can't get to me. So she probably needs a gun too. And lessons."

This was a lie, considering Mom already had a gun. She actually had four. They were Dad's. She also knew how to use them. She wasn't a fan of firearms, as such. It wasn't like it was a hobby. She was just a fan of the second amendment, because she'd been my father's woman for nearly forty years and he was a big fan of firearms as well as, obviously, the second amendment.

Maybe I should have just asked for one of Dad's.

Then again, if I'd asked, it would make her worried about my state of mind.

So I hadn't asked.

The fact that she could, indeed, be on Bounty radar was something I needed to chat with her about.

It was clear I didn't know Beck and his brothers as well as I thought I did.

Now I knew anything was possible.

It was also clear I should have probably gone out shooting with my dad one of the times he'd mentioned it. But this was part of my mom not being a fan, as such. She said Dad could teach me to shoot when I was old enough and when I was old enough I got more interested in shopping, movies, and boys with bikes (not in that order) and I forgot to ask my dad to teach me to shoot.

"Chaos covering her mother?" Zip asked Snapper, taking me out of my thoughts.

"Just get the binder, Zip," Snap ordered on a sigh.

Zip shot a squinty-eyed look at Snap before he grumbled unintelligibly and moved away.

"I'm not sure I want to look at whatever this binder is," I decreed and Snap stopped watching Zip move and looked to me.

"You definitely don't wanna look at Zip's binder," he confirmed.

I decided to change topics.

"This house you all moved me into, is it one of yours?" I asked.

"Yup," he answered without delay, no beating around the bush for Snapper.

"Did you evict someone for me?" I asked.

"Yup," he answered, again without delay.

Holy crap.

He actually had.

"Like, in a day?" I queried, my voice higher, my eyebrows searching for my hairline.

"Gave them two days," he told me.

"That's…well, that's crazy."

"Had another property open. Bigger, nicer, moved them into that. Same rent. So I didn't evict them, exactly. And they had no complaints."

Bigger property, same rent as the smaller one.

And for the time being, I was rent free.

He was going to bleed money for me.

Oh God.

"Snap, you didn't have to do that."

"You're wrong."

"I can stay with Mom until—"

"Rosie, it's done."

I closed my mouth.

Zip showed with the binder.

Snap's leather creaked as he reached out, took it from Zip's fingers, dropped it to the case and opened it at random.

The second my eyes fell on what was inside, I took a step back.

Left side, eight by ten, man on his back in the street, chest covered in blood that came from several holes, eyes open and staring unseeing, since he was very clearly dead.

Gross and creepy.

Right side, eight by ten, man on his side in a gutter, half his skull gone, blood everywhere, brain matter a blood-covered white-gray wodge of goo that wasn't all contained in the place it should be, even more very clearly dead.

Way creepier and off-the-charts gross.

This was a curious thing for a gun shop owner to have.

Unless he was a responsible gun shop owner who wished to impart the seriousness of owning a gun on people like me.

"You got a weapon in your hand, you got the power to do that," Snapper said, tapping a finger sharply on the right-side picture. "You good with that?"

I tore my eyes away and looked to him to see him facing the binder with his gaze aimed over his leather-clad shoulder at me.

Taking him in, for a second, I was thrown off kilter.

When the whole thing started with me informing on Bounty to Chaos, and Snapper was assigned as my Chaos handler, we'd always met in person. I preferred it that way because I knew he'd never approach if he hadn't checked to make sure he could. Telephone conversations could be overheard. Beck had my phone password, so if he got any suspicions and was sneaky about it, without me noticing, texts could be checked.

I didn't want a record. I didn't want evidence easily available. I didn't want to have to hide what I was doing in my everyday life. I wanted Chaos to handle all that for me by casing the area to make sure it was safe to approach.

Okay, so now I realized I also wanted an excuse to see Snapper on a regular occasion. But also it had to do with feeling safe while I was informing on the criminal activities of a motorcycle club.

For some reason, after a while of meeting face to face, Snap decided it would be better if he didn't approach and he gave me a burner. I didn't like it but I figured the Chaos men knew how to do this better to keep it safer for me.

This turned out not to be the case.

In the end, I didn't know how Beck found out. During the tense ride we took before he delivered me to withstand Bounty justice, he didn't share.

But my guess was, since he had that burner, and it didn't have password protection, that was how he'd found out, even though I kept it in my purse, which had been secured in the little staff room at Colombo's.

Snap didn't text. He called. So I couldn't imagine even after Beck found it, he'd know.

Unless he did what I'd guessed he'd done. After they'd been taken down by the cops during one of their runs, Beck somehow started suspecting me, so he'd broken into the staff room, found the burner in my purse, called the only number stored in it, and Snap had answered.

I was curious about this as well as curious about how Snap and Roscoe had known where to find me.

This wasn't what was on my mind at that time, standing in Zip's Gun Emporium with Zip and Snap.

What was on my mind was that it had ended up where Snap and I had a lot of phone conversations that had nothing to do with what was going down with Chaos and Bounty.

We just talked, about everything.

He knew about my mom and dad. He knew I liked my job but mostly the people I worked for. He knew my favorite pastime was shopping but I also liked going to movies and reading.

I knew he got along with his folks, was still tight with his brother and sister, even if he'd found another family in Chaos. I knew he spent a lot of time reading, mostly thrillers (I even knew Steve Berry was his favorite author, he was a Cotton fiend). Having that knowledge, it wasn't a big jump to the fact Snap was also a history buff. So if he wasn't reading, doing Chaos stuff, out on a ride (a lot of the time solitary, even if he found the brotherhood, it was just his way), he watched documentaries.

And we were both *X-Files* fans.

But before we got into the marathon phone conversation drill, we'd met up and he was Snapper. The boy-next-door biker with the easy-to-be-with nature and even easier grin.

He was Chaos so the badass was inherent.

It just had never been apparent.

Right then, the way he held my gaze steady, looking over his leather-clad shoulder, the Chaos patch on the back of his cut, his face set, making a point, the badass was out.

And damn it...

I liked it.

"I would aim to maim," I shared shakily, not feeling very happy about this new way Snap Kavanaugh could affect me.

"Do you have even a little clue how good a marksman you gotta be to aim to maim and do that shit successfully in an uncertain or tense situation?" he asked.

"Marksperson," I muttered.

He turned slowly to me, the badass still brimming from him, vibrating against me, and my determination not to get involved with another biker ever (and definitely imminently) took a hit.

God, why did my dad have to be so awesome?

Why couldn't I be attracted to geeks, metrosexuals, or hipsters?

"Rosalie, this shit is serious," he stated, all steely.

Snapper, easy-to-be-with was great.

Snapper being steely in a gun shop was *fantastic*.

Time to escape.

"I think I need to go home," I mumbled.

"We're goin' for coffee," Snap declared.

"We're not going for coffee," I returned.

"You in a gun shop lookin' to get armed, time I give you space to regroup is done. We need to talk," he told me.

"We don't have anything to talk about anymore."

Steely gone, gentle and sweet in its place, Snap said, "Rosie, there will never be a time when you and me don't have shit to talk about."

Whoa, that was crazy-sweet.

I decided to get mad instead of scared.

Or excited.

"I just got beat to hell by my boyfriend and his brothers," I reminded him.

"You got beat to hell *six days ago* by an asshole I always knew was an asshole but now you know is an asshole, though you already knew it, you just weren't admitting it. And in those six days you've also figured out why you were with him but you still had all the time in the world to have a lotta phone conversations with me."

Direct hit.

Damn.

"Are we gonna do this in front of Zip?" I asked.

"Just to say, if I got a choice, I'd rather you not do this in front of me," Zip put in.

"We're gonna do it wherever we gotta do it so I can be assured you know where I'm at and I got you there with me." Snapper ignored Zip to answer.

"I knew I wouldn't have a choice," Zip mumbled.

"I think I'd rather focus on the fact that Bounty isn't done with me," I shared.

"Bounty is done with you," he retorted.

I wished that was true.

"You know they're not, Snap," I whispered.

"I know one more Chaos woman gets dragged into brother business, Denver is facing Armageddon," Snap replied.

"To move this along," Zip said, and we both looked his way, "I can confirm that too. Streets are full of talk about Bounty bein' pussy and takin' their shit out on a girl. They're also full of Chaos bein' at the end of their tether, and we'll just say things are feelin' seriously uneasy."

"Zip, you wanna butt out?" Snap asked.

"Boy, you're havin' this out with your woman in my store. I don't butt outta shit in my store," Zip returned. "And pay attention, I'm helpin' you out."

"I'm going home," I declared, starting to move past Snapper, but I didn't get far because he caught me with his fingers wrapped around the crook of my elbow.

I looked up at him.

"Baby, let's just get some coffee," he said.

He was right.

I'd needed to regroup.

He was also wrong.

I wasn't done regrouping.

I needed a lot more time.

And right then I had to set about getting it.

"He had the burner," I shared.

Snapper's beautiful lips thinned.

"I wanted to meet," I told him.

"There was a reason I went that way," he whispered. "You have coffee with me, I can explain."

I ignored that offer.

"Did he call you?" I asked.

"No," he answered.

Really?

"He didn't call?" I pushed.

Snapper shook his head.

"How did he know?" I asked.

"You had a burner, honey," he explained.

Just that.

I had a burner and there was no reason for me to have an extra phone.

Unless I was betraying my boyfriend.

Suddenly, this whole thing was worse.

One and one equaled two, of course, but Beck hadn't even ascertained definitively that two was the two they were seeking vengeance for.

He suspected me, located the phone and found me guilty without asking me a question or conclusively establishing my culpability.

It honestly didn't matter that he was right.

What mattered was that he didn't even *ask* before he came to a verdict and sentenced me.

Especially the sentence he'd given me.

"How did you know where to find me?" I asked Snapper.

"Bounty's place to do their wet work is known."

Wet work.

My ex-man and his brothers had a place they did wet work that was known.

Did Chaos have a place they did wet work?

Probably.

I nodded to Snap. "I need to go home."

"They're not gonna get near you or your mom."

I nodded again.

"Let you go now," he gave in, probably reading me, and being Snap, giving that to me because he knew how much I needed it. "But we need to talk, Rosie."

I shook my head.

"Honey—" he began.

I searched for another excuse and fortunately found one.

"I need to grieve my father."

At that, he blinked, ending his blink with his brows aimed high.

"Sorry?" he asked.

"I need to grieve my father," I repeated.

"He died three years ago, Rosie."

"Yes, and it's come clear to me of late that I haven't been dealing with that in a healthy way."

His fingers at my arm curled deeper at the same time he pulled me closer.

"Everett," I said softly, a warning.

"Throttle was not your dad," he told me, demonstrating he knew exactly what I was talking about.

"I know."

"I'm not either."

Yes you are.

And weirdly, that scared me more than anything.

"Please, I need to go," I begged.

"You gotta know you'd never get that shit from me, from Chaos, no matter what you did," he said. "But you wouldn't have to do it 'cause that's not our path."

"What is your path?"

"It's not that," he stated.

We'd finally made it.

We'd made it right at the place I needed to be to get him to leave me be.

And I jumped on it.

I looked him direct in his snow-blue eyes.

"Armageddon takes everyone out, Snapper."

His fingers convulsed on my arm right before I gently pulled it free.

I looked to Zip, gave him a trembling smile and said, "Nice to meet you."

"Come back for a Taser," was his reply.

I nodded, thinking I didn't want to be responsible for someone who was out to harm me losing their brain matter, but I probably would have no issue with amping them significantly.

I then looked to Snap, who was watching me but didn't make another move to detain me, and on unsteady legs, I walked out of the gun shop.

Chapter Three

Crosshairs

Rosalie

I timed it so it worked for me.

I was now ten days out. The bruising was fading faster. I was moving around a lot easier. A new bandage was on my nose and it was a lot smaller. And the stitches were dissolving and falling out.

But I still looked like a woman who'd had her ass handed to her.

Colombo's was being cool. They were giving me time off with pay (though that pay sucked, it was all about the tips) for two weeks and putting me behind the bar until the bandage was off my nose, my stitches were totally gone, and my ribs were such I could heft around huge pizza pies.

So it was now or it would be never.

And too much was at stake.

It couldn't be never.

Even if the now scared the beejezus out of me.

Therefore I was sitting in the room with all the stations, chairs facing each other on either side of a wall that was half glass, partitions delineating the stations.

Phones hanging on a partition at each station.

I watched him come out, and regardless of the fact he looked about as rough as me, and then some, I remembered what I'd thought the first time I saw him in the bar Bounty hung at.

That could be mine.

And I'd made it mine.

He copped a blank look as he moved to me, his big, powerful body no less attractive in an orange jumpsuit with a white T-shirt under it.

And it was proved.

The stitched slash that carved from just below the corner of his inner left eye across his cheekbone then down to his jaw only made him look tough, hot, and cool.

Making the trek from door to sitting opposite me, Beck did not lose hold on my gaze.

Only when I did nothing but sit there, staring at his still-handsome face, did his brown eyes slide to the telephone and back to me.

Now he wanted to talk.

I looked down at my lap where my purse was.

It was a cute purse. Total biker chick chic, black leather in a saddlebag shape with lots of rivets and a fantastic, heavy silver chain as a strap.

Since I was no longer going to be a biker chick, I was probably going to have to switch out my entire purse inventory, finding hipster purses or something like that.

The problem was the very idea of hipster purses made me want to cringe and I didn't even know what a hipster purse looked like.

The sleek clutch Lanie was carrying, I could do.

Hipster…

No.

I stopped thinking of hipster purses, which was just my way of controlling my fingers' need to start trembling because Beck was right across from me and the last time I'd seen him had not been a celebratory occasion. I got myself together and opened my purse.

I pulled out the folded piece of paper. I unfolded the paper, turned it the way I needed it, then slapped it up against the glass off to the side so that Beck could still see my face through the glass.

His gaze went to the paper and I thought he'd keep the blank look, close me off, shut me out, or alternately, sneer.

He didn't do either.

He looked at the color copy of the picture of me before they'd cleaned the blood off my face in the hospital but after the swelling had bloated me beyond recognition and he flinched.

Flinched.

What was that all about?

So abruptly that I jumped in my chair, his big hand came up and curled around the phone.

He yanked it out of the cradle, tapped the top against the glass, gaze back on me, and put it to his ear.

I shoved the picture back into my purse and picked up the phone even though I had meant the picture to speak for me.

That being, *I already paid, leave me alone.*

I put the phone to my ear.

"Rosie."

That was all he said but I heard the tone, I saw the look in his eyes.

The tone was guttural.

The look was suffering.

He had to be kidding me.

"I hate you," I whispered.

His features softened in that way they did when he thought I was being cute or when he wanted to have sex or when I put his favorite meal in front of him or when he wanted me to forgive him for acting like a dick or a thousand other times when I reminded him why he'd made me his old lady or he got himself in trouble with me.

This was not in trouble with me.

As phenomenal as a soft look from Gerard "Throttle" Beck could be, we were far beyond that ever working again on me.

"Rosie—"

"Keep them away from me. From Mom and from me."

"Why did you—?"

I leaned toward the glass and interrupted him. "Too late now, Beck. Too late to ask questions."

"Web said—" he began, I knew to explain.

Web. Spiderweb. Bounty's president.

What I also knew was there was no explanation. Not one I would understand.

The brothers, okay, they were in an outlaw motorcycle club, I knew the risks I was taking.

Him? My man?

There was no explanation.

"Web didn't tell you to choke me. He didn't tell you to hit me."

His face started to get hard. "Baby, you ratted out the club."

"You did your thing. Now keep them away from Mom and from me."

"You shouldn't have reported it to the cops, Rosie."

That was what I was afraid of.

"What'd you think I'd do?" I asked.

"My deal with them was they'd leave you alive. Thought you'd learn to keep your mouth shut," he told me.

"Well, thanks, Beck. So good to know you were looking out for me."

He leaned into the glass. "Baby, Rosie, Christ. *You ratted out the club.*"

"I slept at your side," I whispered.

His gaze fell then came right back up.

I kept at him.

"You could have been the father of my children."

He winced and started, "Rosie—"

"When the club started to roll that way, I should have just left you."

"I wouldn't have let you go."

"You wouldn't have had a choice."

"No, Rose," he growled, "*you* wouldn't have."

That gave me a shiver but I powered through it.

"Then it's all worked out for the best."

That was when the sneer came. "He's married, Rosalie. Got a fuckin' kid. Get over it."

What was he talking about?

"What?" I asked.

"Cage. He's never gonna be yours. He's gone for her and trust me, when that shit happens for a biker, it doesn't turn around."

He was talking about Shy. Shy and Tabby and me.

Ancient freaking history.

And trust him about that kind of thing?

He *totally* had to be kidding me.

"How can I trust you when you have no clue what you're talking about?" I queried.

"Then you weren't paying attention," he snarled, allowing the hurt he felt at my betrayal and my supposed longing for Shy to rise to the surface.

"No, Beck, you weren't. I've been over Shy since that night I rode at your back and you took me to Lookout Mountain and kissed me with the lights of Denver spread out around us."

"Right, that's why you handed us over to Chaos, who handed us to the fuckin' cops."

"No, I did it because when I made a baby with my man, I wanted that baby to know down to his bones his father was a good man in a way the day that father passed from this earth, he'd struggle to cope, but he wouldn't struggle to come to terms with the fact this world was better with his daddy in it."

Beck shut his mouth and did it looking stricken.

That got in there.

Finally.

But still too late.

I did not shut my mouth.

"I wanted you to see how dangerous what you were doing was. How easy it would be for your life to be wasted, the life you shared *with me*. I wanted you to take a good look at it and find a reason to turn yourself around. I tried to talk to you about it, you wouldn't hear me. So I felt the need to do something to save you, save us, to save our future. And unfortunately for both of us, it got to the point where that something had to be extreme."

Beck had nothing to say to that either.

So I kept going.

"Just to say, I wouldn't admit it to myself, but when you refused to listen to my concerns about where the club was going and what that meant to our lives and our future, it ended with us. Long before you left me bleeding and passed out on a cement floor."

He shook his head. "You drop the charges, Rosie, and I'll talk to Web and the guys about letting this shit end here with you."

I nodded my head. "You're gonna talk to Web and the guys and you're all gonna leave me alone."

"You need to drop the charges, Rose."

"If I have to sit in a box and look every one of you in the eye before I put you behind bars, I'll do it."

"Babe—"

I yanked the paper out of my purse and flattened it on the glass.

"My mother saw me like that, Beck."

He turned his head away.

He loved my mom. Practically doted on her. An old lady without her biker. All of Bounty treated her like a dowager queen.

"She *saw* that," I pushed. "*You* made her see me like that."

He turned back to me. "Rosie, we got serious problems because of your bullshit."

I shoved the picture back in my purse, saying, "*I* wasn't caught transporting drugs. *I* didn't abduct my girlfriend from her place of business and deliver her to a warehouse where *me* and the men I call my brothers beat her to shit. *You* and *your brothers* did that."

"You know the code," he bit.

"I do. My father was a biker and he taught me. Woman. Kids. Bike. Freedom. In that order. Where are you now with all of that, Beck?"

"You did it for Cage," he clipped, not letting that stupid crap go.

"No. But I will say, in the beginning, I did it for you, but in the end, I didn't."

His brows shot together. "What the fuck does that mean?"

I wasn't about to explain that one.

"Leave me and Mom alone."

"Boys'd never touch your ma," he muttered.

That was delivered in a mutter but I believed it.

Thank God.

I believed it.

I fought back heaving a gigantic sigh of relief and instead demanded, "Leave *me* alone."

He leaned deeper toward me and got a look on his face that what now seemed long ago would have had me dropping to my knees or flat on my back in a split second.

"Baby, I'm beggin' you, *drop the charges*."

"You didn't ask me."

"Rosalie—"

"You didn't give me the chance to explain."

"Rosie—"

"You *choked me*."

"Rose—"

"And *hit me*."

"Christ, baby—"

"And you *spit on me*."

Beck shut up.

"Then you *kicked me*."

Another flinch.

I stared into his eyes.

He had amazing eyelashes.

He stared into mine.

"I loved you once," I whispered.

Those eyelashes swept down.

Yeah.

Amazing.

"You terrify me now," I told him.

Those eyelashes swept up to reveal tortured eyes.

I knew it then.

He'd been ordered to deliver me to Bounty.

He might also have been ordered to start the proceedings.

But it wasn't until right then that I realized that he'd done what he'd done in the beginning, and at the end, but in the middle, it was his brothers that brought down their version of justice on me.

He'd given them their show and he didn't come back for more because he'd done as ordered and that was all he had in him when it came to me.

The parting shots were probably because he was pissed at me, worked up from watching his brothers lay me out, thinking I was hung up on Shy, possibly all of that.

Or still toeing the line.

There were leaders and there were followers.

But even if you were a follower, it was your job to find the right thing to follow and not to follow blindly.

Beck had failed at both.

"The only reason I can be here is because there's a cop right there and a wall between us," I shared, jerking my head toward the officer that stood by the door into the visitation room. "If you ever cared about me, keep them away from me."

"I love you, baby, still, no matter what, you gotta know that," he said into the phone quietly.

"Weirdly, someone chokes me, hits me, spits on me, and kicks me, that is something I do not know."

"Drop the charges and we'll get through this."

We'll get through this?

Was he crazy?

"Leave me alone, get your brothers to leave me alone, and I might not hate you until the day I die," I countered.

"Rosie—"

"We're done."

"Rosie, baby—"

"You're one of the most beautiful men I've ever seen," I whispered the God's awful truth.

He clamped his mouth shut again.

"And you made me happy, so unbelievably happy."

His brown eyes lit and warmed.

"And then you didn't."

Despair flickered in his gaze before he dropped his head.

"Do you know one of the reasons why my father never joined a club?" I asked.

He lifted his head but said nothing.

"He wasn't a man to be tied down, but that wasn't all there was to it," I shared something I'd told him before, but at this juncture, a reminder was deserved. "Most clubs expect you to put club before everything else, including your family, your old lady. And he just was not a man who could do that."

"I'm not your daddy, Rosie," he said gently.

"I know," I replied, put the phone on the hook decisively and watched his face falter.

That was the last I gave him.

I got up, dragged the silver chain of my purse over my shoulder, and walked out.

The minute I went through the door, I stutter-stepped because there was a tall, exceptionally good-looking man built like a linebacker leaning against the wall of the hall outside. He had a badge on his belt and his whisky-brown eyes turned to me the minute I exited.

I'd never seen him in my life but I still sensed his gaze was apologetic.

The door swung closed and those whisky eyes shifted across the hall, taking mine with them, and that was when I stopped altogether.

Snap was there, hidden by the door but now revealed.

"Thanks, Nightingale," he muttered half a second before he latched onto my hand and dragged me down the hall, turned and hauled me down another one, through reception and out the front doors.

He wasn't done lugging me around because he then rounded on me and started forward, forcing me to walk backward, until my hips hit the railing at the side of the steps up to the station.

He then bent his neck so his face was an inch from mine and I saw his snow-blue eyes *could* be chilly.

Wintry cold with icy fury.

"Have you...lost...*your mind*?"

The first words were controlled, but barely.

His last two were nearly shouted.

"Snapper," I whispered.

"What the fuck were you thinking?" he demanded to know.

"You need to step back," I told him.

"Oh no," he drawled ominously, actually moving forward so his hips were pressed to my belly, his chest brushing my breasts and his frosty eyes filling my vision. "Oh no, baby. Ol' Snap's done with givin' his woman some space."

"I'm not...your woman," I said hesitantly, like I didn't believe my own words.

"How old am I?" he asked.

"Thirty-three," I answered immediately and uncomprehendingly, bemused by his question in the midst of what was happening.

"My favorite color?" he pressed.

"Red."

"How do I take my coffee?"

I'd learned that early, when he'd come into Colombo's and have some cannoli and a cup of joe, before my informant status heated up.

"Lotsa cream, one sugar."

"My favorite book?"

"*Shutter Island*."

"You're twenty-eight. Your favorite color is green. You take your coffee with just creamer, vanilla if it's handy. Your favorite book is *Harry Potter*, the Azkaban one, and you flirted for a good long while with convincing yourself you could get away with naming your first girl Hermione."

I shook my head, baffled where this was going. "I don't—"

"You want two kids, because you wished you had a sister or brother, at least, and you want to start as soon as you can, because your dad was older than your mom and she wasn't young when she had you and you lost him way too early for both of you, even though he was in his seventies."

"I—"

"You've lived everywhere bikers are welcome on this side of the Mississippi but your favorite was always Denver, the three times your daddy moved you and your mom here. It was his favorite too, because he loved to ride the Rockies. And that was the only thing that gave you and your mom any relief when he passed, that you could take him up to the mountains when his time had come and he went somewhere he loved being."

"Snap," I said softly.

"You're done with comic hero movies. You think Dwayne Johnson would kill in a romantic comedy. You like to vacation at beaches. Your favorite cookie is a snickerdoodle. Your favorite restaurant is Carmine's. You're uncertain about the death penalty seeing as you're a conservative liberal, but in deference to your father, you've convinced yourself you're a liberal conservative. And your favorite place in the whole world is riding on the back of a bike."

Boy, I'd talked a lot during our phone conversations.

And Snap had listened closely.

He wasn't quite finished with me.

"Only thing you don't know about me that means anything is the way my cock feels buried inside you and only thing I don't know about you is how sweet you'll feel, closed tight around me."

Oh man.

That sweet he'd feel started for me to feel tingly.

"Snapper," I whispered.

"And you're not my woman?"

"I—"

"You been my woman for months and I don't give a shit that happened when you were with another man."

It was me shutting my mouth during this conversation.

"And you just visited that man in jail, a man that delivered a beat down that put you in the goddamned hospital," he stated infuriatedly.

"I was warning him off me," I explained.

He dipped the half an inch he needed for the tip of his nose to brush mine (something it did).

"Rosalie, I'll repeat, *that motherfucker is not gonna touch you.* Not *ever* a-fuckin'-*gain.*"

"You good, hoss?"

Snap's head jerked around. I looked past his shoulder. And there stood two uniformed officers who weren't real thrilled a man in a motorcycle cut with his colors stitched to the back had a woman pinned to the railing outside a police station.

"Snapper. Chaos. This is Rosalie. The woman Bounty beat to shit. She just visited Throttle to warn him off. She's mine. I didn't know she was up to that shit. And we're havin' a discussion about how that doesn't make me happy."

Masculine understanding dawned in both officers' eyes. One gave Snapper a chin lift and moved toward the front door. The other gave him a look of beleaguered male camaraderie and then he moved toward the front door.

I tracked them, losing both between Snapper's broad shoulders, getting them back only to lose them again when the men and the coffees they were carrying disappeared inside the police station.

Did that just happen?

"Rosie," Snapper growled.

My eyes drifted back to him.

"We need to talk," he declared, *again.*

"I'm not ready for that."

"I'm sorry, baby, but I no longer give a shit."

Now it was me who was getting angry.

"Are you serious?" I asked.

"Rosalie, you just visited fuckin' *Throttle* in jail."

"Yes, to tell him to leave me and Mom alone!" I snapped.

"Right, let me explain this to you thoroughly," he bit back. "Communication between you and any member of Bounty, *especially* Throttle, is done. Over. Not fucking happening. There's a message to deliver, Chaos delivers it. If they already haven't learned that you've ceased to exist, we'll share that with them as many times as we got to until they *get it.* You have nothing to fear from them because every brother who's earned the Chaos patch will go down before they hurt you again. You don't have to do dick to make that happen, the brotherhood will bleed themselves dry for you to make you safe. Now, are you getting me?"

"I—"

He cut me off before I could say more.

"Before you get worked up any of that shit will happen, Tack has gotten word to Web that we know they got a beef, they can't be under any impression other than the fact we feel after what they did to you that we got a beef, but how that's gonna work out is however it works out between *brothers*. Women are off limits, you've been claimed by Chaos, and if dick happens to you, or your mom, it isn't gonna make it a bigger beef. It's gonna be Chaos declaring war and they're vulnerable, so they got this shot bein' incarcerated to get their shit together or we'll dismantle their charter. Now you getting me?"

"Whoa," I whispered.

"You're getting me," he muttered.

"How would you even do that?" I asked curiously.

"With surgical precision, considering Tack's already reached out to other Bounty charters' presidents sharing Chaos and its allies will not be best pleased another woman gets caught in the crosshairs and he's gonna expect a definitive indication from the other charters they're frowning on Bounty's bullshit. To say Bounty, who have never been one percenters, aren't real thrilled Web took their shit in its current direction is an understatement. Might not stop the locals but they'd have their patches stripped, and no biker who's earned his patch doesn't take that seriously. They'd have to start from fresh without a single ally, which is like a newborn baby taking on a full grown bear."

"It, uh…seems you all have this in hand," I mumbled, and that got me the fascinating show of his fabulous lips surrounded by his blond beard twitching.

"Yeah, and if you'd had coffee with me a coupla days ago, I coulda shared a few things and saved you this trip."

Hmm.

"You gonna have coffee with me now?" he asked.

"Um…" I darted my eyes side to side, saying, "I probably should get home. Mom doesn't know I'm here. She went to the grocery store for her weekly huge-ass shop and since this is lasting longer than I expected, she might be back before I get home and she's a little…" I searched for a word, "*troubled* about all the stuff that's swirling around me."

"I bet she is," he said quietly.

"So I should go home," I reiterated.

"When you movin' into my place?" he asked.

"I'm under the impression I'm already moved in."

"I mean, bodily."

There was something about Snapper saying the word "bodily" that also made parts of me tingle.

I refused to get caught up in the tingle.

"Didn't all you just said mean I don't really need the fullness of the protection you and Chaos are offering me?" I asked.

"You think me or any of the brothers are leavin' dick to chance with our women, you'd be thinkin' wrong."

Of course.

"Snap—"

"I know you love spending time with your mom but it'd probably help her out to know you're doin' better in your head that you move back into your life."

This was probably true.

I huffed out a big sigh.

He wrapped a hand around the side of my neck, thumb extended under my chin to push it up.

It was a sweet touch and a cool move.

More tingling.

Damn.

"I'll move in tomorrow," I said.

"Good," he replied.

"Or the next day," I went on.

The look in his eyes that had turned to snowy goodness shifted back to frosty annoyance.

"Rosie, tomorrow," he ordered. "You get in, settle in, we'll talk."

I huffed out another big sigh.

"Face is lookin' good," he muttered, reading accurately from my sigh I was giving in. "How're your ribs?"

"Healing," I muttered back.

"Glad to hear it, Rosie."

The snowy goodness was back in his eyes and a different kind of goodness was in his voice.

I needed to be careful.

"I can't believe those cops just let you keep me pinned to this railing," I remarked.

"Cops aren't big fans of a woman beat to shit by eight motherfuckers," he educated me.

"No one really is," I educated him.

"They're also not big fans of those women waltzing up to one of the assholes who did that shit to have a futile conversation," he shared.

"I didn't know it was futile," I told him.

"I did and they did and fortunately now so do you."

I decided to shut up again.

"Colombo's bein' cool with you?" he asked.

I nodded.

"Baby?" he called.

"Mm?" I answered.

His thumb swept along my jaw. "Go home to your mom before I lose the fight I got goin' with the urge to take you home with me."

Man, I wanted to go home with him.

No you don't! my mind screamed. *Get it together, Rosalie!*

"Maybe we should have coffee, Snapper. There might be a few things you need to get straight too."

He shook his head, his thumb now drawing circles on the hinge of my jaw that caused reciprocal circles to be felt around both my nipples, and I started kicking myself I didn't sprint to my car the minute he told me to go home.

"Unh-unh, coffee's off the table," he declared. "You're settled in, we're havin' dinner."

I then shook *my* head. "I'm not going out to dinner with my face like this."

"I didn't say we were goin' out."

Uh-oh.

"Snap—"

"Go home."

"Snap!"

He bent in, pressing his lips to mine.

I felt those lips and the whiskers of his beard whispering against my skin and I smelled him and I had to clench my hands not to reach out and grab him like a child reaching to grasp hold of a candy bar that was not good for them but they had to have.

It was our first kiss.

Well, kind-of kiss, it wasn't gung ho.

Still, it was a kiss and even not gung ho, stupid, stupid Rosalie, I wanted more.

And because he was wonderful, awesome Snapper, not pushing it outside the press that ended in a soft brush of lips and whiskers, he pulled away and whispered, "Go home to your mom, Rosie."

I nodded because that was a really good idea.

"Talk to you later," he said.

"Right," I replied and nearly cleared my throat but the damage was done, it had come out husky.

He grinned, swept my jaw with his thumb the other way, then stepped back.

I started to sprint to my car but stopped myself before I got in that first rush because I didn't want him to see me doing it.

Once I made it to the bottom of the steps, though, I should have stopped myself from looking back because badass Snapper had come to the fore. He was standing at the top of the steps with his arms crossed on his chest and his eyes on my ass.

Me being with Beck, he'd been holding back.

Now that the floodgates had been opened, he wasn't going to do that anymore.

I thought I had problems but I had a feeling I'd been tossed out of the frying pan only to land in the fire.

I should have sprinted.

I decided to skip trot like I was semi in a hurry but hoping he thought it was because I wanted to get back to Mom before she worried.

There were two good parts to me doing that. One, it got me to my car faster and two, it didn't hurt my ribs too much so I had indication I'd be good to go soon with carting around trays full of food and beverage.

I'd hit my car, had the key in the ignition and was about to turn it on when my phone chimed with a text.

Thinking it was Mom, home to find me gone, and worried about me, I grabbed it.

It was a number I didn't have programmed in, local, and I didn't have to wonder who it was because the text said, *You're so fucking cute.*

Snapper and I didn't have each other's real phone numbers.

Now, we did.

I felt instantly that life was right again after months, no…years of feeling it was all wrong.

Yes, I had problems.

Because I'd fallen in love with a biker who'd dumped me.

Then I fell in love with a biker who went outlaw and then laid the smackdown on me.

And now I was in love with a biker who knew where another club did their wet work, was threatening war against that club, but was already at war with a baddie that set his Club to breaking the biker code and working with cops in order to use another club to take that baddie out.

I might be out of one set of crosshairs (maybe).

But everybody remotely involved with Chaos was in the other.

And that scared the hell out of me.

Chapter Four

Paint

Rosalie

"This place is *so cute*," Mom practically squealed.

I stood in the living room of the house Snap and Chaos moved me into.

She was not wrong.

It was cute.

Clean, cozy, cute.

And *gorgeous*.

It also smelled faintly of paint.

Which meant they'd painted it between Snapper's renters moving out and them moving me in so that they could move me into a pad that was fresh and felt new.

I touched my couch, which had its back to the door and was facing a freestanding fireplace, allowing my head to move slowly around to take in the space.

Beck and I had lived in a nice apartment complex in Aurora. It had some personality but it was a modern complex, built within the last ten years. Not exactly an architectural masterpiece or having had the time to be quaint or historically appealing or having so much of its style demolished around it that it was now unusual.

This place of Snapper's was obviously an old carriage house that sometime along the way had the mansion it had been attached to disappear.

It also had been added on to.

Giving it a sense of privacy and serenity, it was set far back from the curb, much farther back than the other houses on the block, seeing as it once sat behind the house it had served.

It now, amusingly, since it used to be the same thing, had a large two-car garage with the doors of the garage facing the side of the property so the garage looked like an extension of the little house, not a monstrosity of what was essentially storage space almost as big as the living space it had been tacked onto.

The garage was accessed through the kitchen.

We'd walked in the front door.

And the front door led to a living room that was relatively spacious, but definitely well lit with an abundance of beautiful, old-fashioned, multi-paned windows at the front and side of the house.

The walls were creamy white and had my Toulouse-Lautrec prints and other wall stuff already up on them. My flat screen had been mounted on the creamy-painted brick above the freestanding fireplace. And that fireplace was set in a wall of that brick that sat in the middle of the living room with a spiral staircase off to the side.

My furniture, that was in yellows (couch) and denims (armchair and some of the toss pillows on the couch), which I'd always thought was awesome, but had never looked like much in the pad I shared with Beck, looked amazing against the buttery-white walls and the hardwood floors (though I now needed a rug).

To the left, there was a dining area that led off from a kitchen (which meant I also needed a dining room table).

The hardwood floors stretched everywhere, including the kitchen that was open to the space entirely, didn't even have an island or bar. But the big window at the back, the pearly-tiled backsplash, the window-fronted, milky-painted cupboards and the uninterrupted space made it seem bright, crisp and airy, but also warm and welcoming. All this juxtaposed with some sharply angled parts of the ceiling just made it interesting.

I wandered the kitchen then came out and moved between the fireplace and the spiral staircase. I saw a little alcove at the back that was somewhat roomy but mostly snug that could be a reading nook. But Chaos (or their old ladies) had set it up with my desk and laptop, making it my office.

And again, my white, sectional corner desk with its long arm and the kickass wicker rolling chair I'd found hadn't seemed like much in Beck and my extra bedroom in our apartment, but there it looked crazy-cool.

Also, with the desk fit into the corner and down the wall, I could still fit an armchair and ottoman in there, making it a dual-purpose space, adding the little reading nook.

Some of this space was an addition, definitely the powder room I saw through an open doorway at the back.

I knew this because it jutted out past the kitchen and had French doors at the side aimed toward the corner of the jut made from mini-den and kitchen that created a little courtyard.

This was covered in a vine-festooned pergola. It had a wood deck and some big glossy pots, but since it was February, there was nothing much there. However, in the summer it could be a riot of flowers interspersed with the garden furniture I right then decided to buy, a little piece of outside tranquility in the heart of the city.

"Rosalie?" Mom called.

I drifted down the kind of hall formed by the wall of the kitchen and the fireplace, back through the living room, and up the spiral stairs.

I stopped right at the top.

The ceilings were low, beamed, some of them angled, all painted that creamy white.

And in a dormer sat a beautiful scroll-backed, king-size bed covered with white and yellow bedclothes.

None of that mine.

Beck and I had a queen-size bed, and from what I could tell, Chaos had cleaned out our apartment so if he ever got out of jail, he'd come back to it empty.

Except our bed.

Even as I wandered the bedroom area that covered the entire house (outside the sharp eaves that cut into the space, but even so, they made it all the more awesome), I stared at that bed until I hit the master bath that was not enormous but it did have a crazy-cool soaking tub and a double-bowled vanity.

Through that was a walk-in closet that had one wall slanted but ran the length of the house. The other wall was filled with shelves, rods and drawers. It wasn't every woman's fantasy closet but it was better than I'd had and would more than do the trick.

"Rosie," Mom said softly.

She'd entered the closet with me.

My clothes were hanging there.

I opened a drawer to find my panties, closed it and stared at a shelf where my collection of enameled jewelry boxes had been arranged.

"Honeypot."

It was a one-bedroom house, essentially.

But it had been entirely renovated and it had been that beautifully. It had a two-car garage and a huge front yard. It was in a good part of Denver. So the rent was probably, but deservedly, crazy.

What could Snap possibly have to give the renters to lure them out of here?

Mom's hand fell on my arm and I finally looked at her.

"Are you okay?" she asked.

"That's not my bed," I told her.

"I know," she said carefully.

"He didn't want the bed I slept in with Beck here," I shared. "So he bought me a new one."

She said nothing, just studied me.

"A really *nice* new one," I went on.

"I'm not sure what you want me to say," she replied.

"Did he do that for me or for him?" I asked.

"I don't know, honeypot. I've never met him."

Knowing Snap, it was for me, and him getting something out of it was ancillary.

"They repainted," I declared.

"I could tell," she said.

"He has other properties," I informed her.

"Okay." She got closer. "Rosalie, why are you freaked?"

"Because he keeps getting better and better and I can't have him."

She got even closer and coaxed gently, "Explain again why you can't have him."

"Chaos is in a mess right now."

"Messes get cleaned up."

"This one is messier than most."

"Rosalie—"

She stopped talking when we both heard the front door open.

I got tense.

Mom got tense along with me.

That could be anyone. Snapper. A random Bounty who'd miraculously made bail and followed us there. A serial killer who happened onto a perfect opportunity.

"Yo!" a man's voice yelled.

I didn't think a serial killer or a random Bounty with revenge on his mind would shout "Yo."

Though I didn't know who that "Yo" belonged to, except it didn't belong to Snapper.

I relaxed.

Mom grabbed my hand, led me out to the bedroom, and preceded me down the winding stairs.

As we went around the curves, standing inside the front door we saw a pretty woman with a mass of goldish-brown curly hair holding a huge vase arranged with roses and berries and branches with leaves on them dripping with some kind of small citrus fruit.

With her was a Chaos man in his cut with a toddler attached to his hip, and dangling from his free hand were about five plastic grocery bags.

"Hi!" the woman cried. "You must be Rosalie and Renae."

"Gah, goo, gee!" the toddler shrieked right before he punched his biker in his bearded jaw and carried on, "Joe-joe-*kah*!"

With obvious practice withstanding the blows, the Chaos brother didn't even flinch after he got struck by the baby. He just watched us alight from the foot of the stairs.

"Yes, this is Rosalie and I'm her mom, Renae," Mom introduced, moving toward them.

"I'm Carissa, and this is Joker and Travis, Joker being the big boy, Travis the little one," the woman replied.

Joe-joe-kah.

Adorable.

My heart hurt.

"Hi, Carissa," Mom said.

"Yes, hi, Carissa," I chimed in. I looked to the brother. "Joker."

"Yo," he grunted.

"Snapper told us you were moving in today so we ran to LeLane's to get you some stuff so you'd feel welcome and are all good to settle in without having to run any errands or anything," Carissa explained, lifting up the arrangement. "We have more in the car. We'll just get it in, put it away, and get out of your hair."

"No," I said swiftly, touched in a totally blown-away sense that they'd do this.

I mean, I liked shopping but not the grocery kind, and I'd never seen anything like that arrangement. It was phenomenal.

Not to mention, they'd gone to LeLane's, which was insanely expensive.

"You should stay for a drink or something." I shot her a smile. "I mean, you can hang with Mom while I pop out to grab some beverages and then you can stay for a drink."

"You're Snap's so bought beer," Joker declared.

I felt my eyes get big at his short declaration that was still uttered like he was reciting what was carved into stone as I heard Mom emit a strangled giggle.

"And I'm a girl and I know not all girls drink beer, so I got you some diet pop and wine," Carissa put in.

"That's perfect!" Mom exclaimed excitedly, a biker babe of the highest order, in other words, always up for company, and taking that further, if any form of alcohol was available, making "company" into a party.

But I was watching Joker and Travis, the former of whom had shifted to look out the windowed front door, the latter of whom was bouncing on his biker's hip, clapping clumsily and squealing, "Hi-ha-hi-ha-hi-ha!"

This was explained when Joker shifted further, getting out of the way of the door just in time for me to see High, another Chaos brother (this one I knew) reaching out to open it. He then came through it trailed by a curvy brunette in a fabulous sweater dress that made me decide I needed a sweater dress (or seven), even more fabulous high-heeled boots, and a gorgeously tailored long wool coat.

I was stunned speechless due to the fact High was carrying an enormous white and black striped bag with tufts of red tissue paper coming out of the top of it.

One of my favorite sights in all the world…carried in by a burly biker.

A Sephora bag.

With reaching arms, Travis grunted his desire to be turned over to High.

With easy expertise, High took the toddler at the same time he kept hold of whatever heaven was in that black and white striped bag.

"Oh no," the brunette said through this. "We're too late to leave our surprise for you."

"Rosalie," High rumbled.

"Hey, High," I greeted. "This is my mom, Renae."

He dipped his chin to Mom and she said, "Hey."

He then grunted, "My woman, Millie."

How long had it been since Neanderthal times?

A week?

"Hey there," Millie called.

Mom and I said our return heys.

"Gonna put this shit in the kitchen," Joker mumbled.

"Carson!" for some reason Carissa snapped, walking toward my coffee table to put down the vase but doing it glaring at her man.

He looked down at the child High was carrying while still moving toward the kitchen.

"Do you know what 'shit' means?" he asked.

"Goo-dee-la-la-kee-la-gee-jah," the kid answered.

Joker looked to Carissa. "That means no."

Carissa turned to Millie and rolled her eyes.

Mom started giggling again.

"How you doin'?" High boomed and suddenly the slightly warm, slightly awkward impromptu welcome wagon party changed to just awkward.

"I'm good, High, thanks," I replied.

His eyes narrowed on my face, taking in the still-angry marks on my brow and jaw and the still-taped nose and he gave clear indication he did not agree with my assessment.

"Let's drink wine," my mother suggested. "Did you girls bring Rosalie's wineglasses over?"

"Of course. We took everything but the asshole's stuff," Millie declared then said quickly toward Carissa, "I mean, the a-hole's stuff."

She turned back to me as she got close to her man and took the Sephora bag from him.

And it was just what I *didn't* want to know about Chaos. Precisely the fact that the brothers in it wouldn't even allow their women to carry Sephora bags, even big ones like that.

Once she'd nabbed it, she lifted it up my way and said, "We girls got together and got you a bunch of housewarming goodies. Have you tried the Moroccanoil line?"

And there it was.

Indication that the old ladies in Chaos understood what "housewarming" meant and it didn't have to do with buying someone a plant.

"No," I told her.

"Oh my *God*," she rhapsodized. "It's *amazing*. We got you the body gel and the body soufflé and the shimmering body oil. Then we got you the Fresh sugar face polish and rose face mask and hydration cream in case you want to do a facial. It's *sublime*. And—"

"Babe, just hand her the bag," High interrupted, having straightened from putting Travis on the floor.

Her head swung High's direction and she gave him a pointy look. "Don't interrupt me while I'm talking about Sephora purchases," she snapped.

High totally ignored her, but did it appearing faintly amused, and looked to me. "You in or you got shit you need to carry in?"

"We just did the walk through so—" I started.

"Right, keys," he ordered, lifting a hand toward me.

"Still got groceries out there," Joker muttered, strolling through the living room toward the front door, glancing down at the baby who was hightailing it to the kitchen, diapered booty wriggling, likely to crawl around the kitchen like he'd do at any trusted friend's house.

Oh man.

"I'll get Rosie's stuff upstairs then help you, Joke," High muttered back as I grabbed my car keys from where I'd tossed them on a table they'd put by the door (that used to be in my foyer in my apartment, but looked *so much better* by that door) and gave them to High.

"Think I can get it all with this go," Joker replied.

He thought?

How many groceries did they buy me?

High took off after Joker before I could ask.

Millie handed me the Sephora bag and prompted on a big smile, "Dig in. Hope you enjoy," before she moved toward the kitchen, Carissa, and rustling grocery bags.

"Gee, tee, dee, la?" Travis asked, and I looked that way to see Mom somehow had hold of him and he was asking her questions.

"I don't know," she answered. "But wanna go see the office space?"

"Dee la!" he agreed enthusiastically.

Watching her wander off with Travis, my heart started hurting again.

"Isn't this place so neat?" Carissa called from the kitchen. "Joker told me that Snapper did the whole design for the reno, though I think that he asked Tyra to help with the fittings. She told me about the awesome tub upstairs and when I saw it the other day when we were moving you in, I swear, I almost ordered everyone out so I could take a bath."

"I have the coolest house on the planet but after I saw that tub, I told Logan we're yanking out ours and getting a soaking one," Millie said.

I watched them putting away groceries.

Then I got out of the path of Joker bringing more in and High carrying my suitcases upstairs.

Mom wandered back in, carrying on a full-blown conversation with Travis.

"Is there any special place you want the bread, Rosalie?" Carissa called and I started out of the frozen trance I seemed to have fallen into.

"I should help you," I replied, beginning to move that way.

"No," Millie denied. "Take a load off and go through your Sephora stash."

"Can I take Travis upstairs?" Mom asked Carissa. "Give him the full tour."

"He was here when we moved Rosalie in, but he loved it upstairs, so absolutely," Carissa answered.

I felt the strings of the Sephora bag I was holding give way from my fingers and I turned to see a returned High setting it on the table by the door.

"Need a word, darlin'," he said.

I looked up at him and nodded.

He put a hand to the small of my back and oddly led me down the hall-type area to the French doors to the courtyard.

Once there, he led me out of them.

It was Denver. It was February. It could be below freezing. There could be a blizzard.

Or it could be like it was that day. Fifty-three degrees.

I still shivered a little bit when High closed the door on us, giving us privacy.

I wasn't sure what was happening out in the courtyard with High.

What I was sure of was that I was *freaking out.*

Snapper owned this crazy-awesome little house.

He'd also apparently fixed it up before he'd had it painted prior to moving me in.

Further, he'd bought me a bed.

But my furniture looked awesome there, like it was bought to be just there.

Not to mention his family had not only moved me in, they got me groceries and a Sephora bag full of happy surprises.

After my father died, I had been looking for something that he'd given me all my life and it wasn't just the stability of his love and pride.

It was his capacity to judge a person's character and his utter refusal to allow anyone in his life, or his girls' lives, who he didn't deem deserved their place there.

He'd been devastated when, back in the day, Chaos had gone from running a garage and growing and selling (then illegal) pot to transporting drugs and firearms through town and pimping women.

He'd been thrilled when the Club had ousted Crank, someone Dad had always hated (and he wasn't a hater, if he didn't like you, he just didn't like you, he didn't detest you—but he'd detested Crank) and Tack had taken his place and cleaned up the Club.

And now here this all was, in my new house where I hadn't even sat my ass down on the couch. Goodness, the kind that Dad had always given me, and more, Dad would always want for me.

Goodness that it was now Snapper who was giving it to me.

"Rosalie," High called my attention to him.

"Yeah?" I asked absently.

He was watching me closely. "You good?"

I shook my head, not in the negative, to pull myself together. "Yes, yeah. I…it's just that a lot is happening."

"Then I'll get this over with, get you inside so you can have a drink, get warm and start settlin' in."

Okay, now I was focused on why High and I were weirdly out in the courtyard for privacy.

"Uh…" I mumbled.

"It was me," he stated. "Snap wanted on you. He wanted to meet face to face. I fucked up. Made a piss-poor call. I was worried that he was meetin' face to face with you because he was into you, which he was and is, but you had a man so I thought he'd get his heart broke. I also worried that Bounty was entering territory they weren't used to dealin' with. I provided security back in the day when Chaos did stupid shit, and when I did, I'd keep an eye on everything. Even old ladies. I thought he'd get caught with you or someone would see you together and inform on you, and I thought you'd be safer, communications were not in person, but he'd also be safer, not fallin' deeper into it spending time with you."

I had to admit, it was good to know why that had happened.

And I didn't want to admit, but I had to do it, that having High confirm what Snapper had already made very clear, that he'd been into me a long time, was more than good.

But now that I knew why, and the why was that why, it didn't matter.

More, I didn't like the idea that these guys were kicking themselves about something that, bottom line, wasn't their fault.

Yes, they'd promised to protect me.

But I had to pull my head out of my ass and get over the fact that what happened was not about them not doing that.

It was about the choices I made, the choices Beck made, and the choices Bounty made.

The Chaos brothers did the best they could do.

The rest was not on them.

"It wasn't you who beat the hell out of me, High. You didn't fuck up."

"Snap woulda kept a closer eye on you if I hadn't warned him off."

"He couldn't be with me twenty-four, seven and have the job get done," I pointed out. "None of you could."

"We fucked up," he reiterated.

"You didn't fuck up."

"You were at work and Speck was on you and we covered you in transit or when you were at your ma's or shoppin' or shit like that. We also kept an eye on Bounty to be sure they weren't making you. We couldn't be on you when you were with Throttle because eventually, he'd see. But Speck was supposed to do drive-bys of the restaurant and since the bust went down and you didn't get outed, he thought you were safe so he went and got himself some tail from a girl he's seein' and didn't stay on you or alternately keep tabs on Throttle. He thought you were at the restaurant, you'd be safe, and he knew when your shift ended and he'd see you home. We also had no warning Bounty clued in on what you'd been doin'."

"High, seriously, *this isn't on you*. It's not on Speck. It's not on Roscoe. It's not on Snap. Being with Throttle, you couldn't keep an eye on me every second of every day and I knew that. I also knew the risks I was taking and I got caught. I informed on an MC to what is now a rival MC. The cops were involved. This is not okay in the world I was living in and I knew that. I still did it, I understood what I was doing, and I knew if I was found out I'd have to deal with some unhappy bikers."

"We were supposed to have you covered."

"That was an impossible task."

I barely got that out before the door opened and we both looked that way, me with my heart shooting straight up in my throat and lodging there because I thought it would be Snapper.

But it was Tack's head that was through the door.

"All good here?" he asked.

"Yes," I answered quickly and firmly before High could say anything.

Tack looked from me to High to me and back to High.

"Tyra and Lanie are here and they're not feelin' wine, they're feelin' cosmos. Joke and Carissa didn't get the shit for that, or any tequila, and Hop doesn't drink the kind of beer they got so I'm doin' a run. You two want anything?"

Tyra, Hop, and Lanie were there too.

And Tack was doing a liquor run.

"What kinda beer did Joke get?" High asked before I could process the idea that apparently, Chaos was throwing me a spontaneous housewarming party.

"Fat Tire," Tack answered.

"Coors," High grunted.

"Right," Tack said then looked at me. "Rosie?"

"I, uh…"

"Memory serves, you're a Corona Light girl," Tack noted.

His memory served correctly.

But a profound hugeness started weighing on me that he remembered at all.

"That or Blue Moon," I whispered.

"Get both," he muttered. "Later."

With that his head disappeared.

I stared at the pretty French doors that led to the pretty mini-den in a pretty house where I was now living that was currently filled with a lot of really good people.

"Rosalie."

I did not look at High.

I turned until I was looking in the kitchen window.

Carissa was there, at the sink, with Tyra.

They were both laughing at something.

Beyond them, Joker had his head back, taking a pull from his beer while Hop was throwing Travis in the air with Mom standing, looking on, clearly giggling up at a giggling Travis.

Millie moved through the space, opening a bag of chips, but stopped when she was met by Lanie, who had another child attached to her hip, and Millie did this so she could tickle and smile into the face of the baby on Lanie's hip.

"Honey," High murmured.

Slowly, I looked to High.

"Did you know my dad?" I asked.

He shook his head. "Before my time."

"He was a good guy."

"Didn't know him, babe, but heard about him, and everything I heard says you tell it true."

"I miss him right now."

"Darlin'," High whispered.

"He'd be doing the liquor run."

I knew High had read my mood when he murmured, "C'm'ere."

I didn't want to go there. I didn't want to accept what they were offering. I didn't want to have it and know for certain how extraordinary it really was only to fear having it torn away.

But I went there.

High's arms opened before I got there and they closed tight around me the instant I made it there.

Yes.

Just as I feared.

It was extraordinary.

Except for the tears I'd shed into the lining of Snap's cut, I had not cried once since Bounty did their number on me.

And except for the tears I'd shared with Mom in the weeks that passed after we lost Dad, I had not cried for him either.

So when they tore loose while High held me to his warmth and strength in a courtyard of the pretty little house the man I'd inadvertently fallen in love with had given to me, they *tore loose*.

I sobbed in his arms, holding on to his leather with fingers clenched deep, and I did it for a long time.

Eventually, High shifted in a way I knew he was going to pass me off and I allowed myself to be passed off, thinking I'd be moving into my mother's arms.

More of the scent of leather, but mingled now with the fresh marine notes of soap assailed me as Snapper's arms wrapped around me.

"What?" he asked under his breath.

"Her pa," High answered. "She misses him."

"Right," Snap muttered.

I then heard a door close and knew Snapper and I were alone.

I just kept crying.

After a while, Snap asked, "You want me to take you upstairs so we can lay down?"

He'd said "we."

Man.

"Th-th-they bought me Sephora," I spluttered.

"They bought you what?" he asked.

"S-s-sephora."

"Sephora?"

I nodded, my cheek moving on leather but feeling the threads of the patches on his chest too.

"What's Sephora?" he asked.

"Only the b-b-best s-s-store in the m-m-mall."

There was a smile in his voice when he said, "See the old ladies took care of you."

"I n-n-need Corona," I told him.

"Good Tack's back with that for you," he replied.

He was back?

Jeez.

How long had I been crying?

"And t-tequila," I added.

"How about you stop crying before you get yourself hammered? You can start bawling again after you're hammered," he suggested.

"M-maybe a good idea," I mumbled into his chest, sniffling and pulling myself together.

Though in doing that, I will note, I did not move from his arms.

"I didn't expect them to do the housewarming party thing, honey. But I'm thinking it's not a bad idea," he remarked.

"Mom loves parties and with Dad gone, she doesn't get to socialize as much as she used to."

"Okay."

"She probably could use getting hammered as well," I continued.

"Probably."

"Did you meet her?" I asked.

"Yeah, she's as pretty as you," he answered.

I hated that I'd missed that.

And I was scared about how much I hated missing it.

I sniffled some more, realizing I was curled into his arms but not holding him. Both my arms were cocked in front of me, my knuckles under my ducked chin, all of this tucked tight to his chest.

It felt nice.

"You painted," I murmured.

"Yeah."

"Bought me a new bed."

He didn't reply to that.

I lifted my head only slightly, keeping my cheek pressed to his chest.

"Snap, you bought me a beautiful new bed."

"I like room to move."

That got my head lifted off his chest.

I looked into his eyes.

The snow was melty.

Very nice.

"We still haven't had our conversation," I pointed out.

"We'll have it over dinner tomorrow. Tonight, we're partying."

I could make this deal so I nodded.

"Are you done crying?" he asked.

"I think so," I answered.

"Wanna tell me why High and you were out here alone?" he asked.

"He wanted to claim responsibility for Bounty being assholes. I refused to let him. Tack remembered what kind of beer I drank. Then I lost it," I answered.

His lips curled up. "Seems a plausible route to a crying jag."

My back straightened. "It's thoughtful to remember the kind of beer someone drinks."

"Babe, I hate to shatter the image you got of Tack but a man remembers the kind of alcohol a woman likes for reasons that are really not thoughtful."

"He's got a woman. He's got no need to liquor another one up."

"Now he does that shit outta pure instinct."

All of a sudden, I started giggling and I did it watching Snapper's lips form a big smile.

God, he was handsome.

Being stupid, *stupid* Rosalie in the arms of handsome Snapper, I uncurled my fingers so I could press them to his chest, pressing myself there with them so I fit more perfectly in his arms.

And just to say, I fit pretty perfectly in his arms already.

Those arms closed snugger around me.

"The house is really amazing, Snap," I told him.

"Minute I saw it, thought you'd like it."

I blinked.

Then I stared.

After that, I started freaking again.

"When did you buy it?" I asked.

"Little over a year ago."

"Snap," I whispered.

"Babe, tomorrow night we can get into the heavy. Now we're either gonna make out or go in and get drunk."

I one hundred percent wanted to make out, and in that instant I didn't think that made me stupid, stupid Rosalie at all.

I looked to his lips.

He started chuckling.

I looked to his eyes. "What's funny?"

He dipped his face closer. "Baby, I like that, what you're sayin', but I was joking. I get my mouth on you I'll want it all over you, and the housewarming party will last approximately two more minutes before I throw all their asses out."

"That won't help Mom have a night where she can let her hair down," I noted.

"Yeah," he agreed.

"But I wasn't sure I was saying anything."

"Man tells you he's thinking of making out with you, you look at his mouth, means you want his tongue in *your* mouth."

"My eyes were wandering," I lied.

"Rosie, even before shit started changing with us, you'd stare at my mouth and it wasn't about your eyes wandering."

This I did not find surprising he'd noticed.

He had a crazy-fabulous mouth.

"I'm currently experiencing significant amounts of emotional turmoil," I explained.

"That isn't lost on me."

"And kinda have been for a while."

"And that hasn't been lost on me for a while."

"In fact, I think I need about three months of mellow times before I make any more big life decisions."

"That I can give you."

I found that disappointing.

I also found my mouth asking, "Really?" before I could stop it.

"Trust me, you're gonna find it impossible to be anything *but* mellow after I'm through with that body, and once I get it, I intend to spend as much time working it as I can."

Oh man.

I shivered and in Snap's arms it had nothing to do with standing outside in fifty-degree weather in February.

His brows rode low over his eyes. "You gonna stand here turning me on so I gotta hang out here to get my shit sorted or go in with you and have to adjust my crotch so they don't see my cock is stiff?"

Against my volition, my belly swayed so I could test the validity of this statement.

This statement was valid.

Very nice.

A growly noise slid up his throat.

Crazy nice.

I melted deeper into his arms, running my hands inside his cut and over his pecs.

Also super *nice.*

"I see the answer to my question is yes," he said.

What was I doing?

I halted the progress of my hands.

"I'm not intentionally turning you on," I told him, and that was actually (kind of) true.

"Baby, watched you do your skip-jog to your car yesterday and stood on the steps to a cop shop fighting back a hard-on. Essentially you gotta breathe in my vicinity and I'm struggling with a boner."

I started giggling again.

"She thinks it's funny," he murmured.

"Maybe we should go inside," I suggested.

"Definitely you should go inside and get me a beer. I'll be in when I can walk in the door and my dick isn't entering the house before me."

And more giggles.

"Get used to that," he ordered.

"What?" I asked, still laughing.

"A time in your life where you'll spend a lot of it laughing."

Oh *man.*

I stopped laughing.

"Baby," he whispered, "go get your man a beer."

"You want Fat Tire, Coors, or Corona Light?"

His expression shifted like he was hiding something.

And what he was hiding was looking hurt.

"Fat Tire," I said swiftly, having seen him drink that not only at the Compound when I was with Shy, but also order it at Colombo's in the times he was not there to have cannoli and coffee but there to have pizza at the bar and I'd find times to break away and chat with him.

The veil drifted away and Snap was all good again.

It was in that moment I felt it imperative he knew.

So I told him.

"I was as into you as you were into me, Snapper. It was just all messed up then and it's all messed up now."

"Heavy shit tomorrow, honey," he replied.

I nodded.

"Beer," he reminded me.

I nodded again, started to pull at his arms but then stopped and rolled up on my toes to touch my lips to his before I pulled free and went in to get Snap's beer.

The lip touch was about Sephora.

It was about Joe-joe-kah.

It was about the bed.

It was about Corona Light.

And also about tequila.

It was about the laughter.

And the tears.

It was about the house.

But oddly, most of all…

It was about the paint.

Chapter Five

Dawn

Rosalie

The sun was shining when my eyes opened.

So it was a sun-washed, tanned, defined, partially tatted male torso that my eyes hit the instant they opened.

I knew where I was.

I was in my new bed in the carriage house pressed down the side of Snapper.

And I knew why I was there.

I'd scratched the surface of precisely how extraordinary being a part of Chaos was.

But more, I'd dug deeper into just how extraordinary having Snapper in my life could be.

To say Carissa and Joker had filled my cupboards was an understatement. It was a wonder the kitchen didn't sink down into the foundations a foot, it was groaning so much from food.

We made a dent in it eating chips and dip and sandwiches and drinking beer and wine, cosmos and tequila shooters (I just had beer).

It was all fine and dandy until (what it did not take very long to learn was) a hilarious woman named Elvira came over with her incredibly handsome fiancé Malik and then all hell broke loose when she and Mom talked the other women into playing quarters on my coffee table.

I decided to hang on the floor in the corner by the stairs with Snap and Joker, letting Travis and Nash (Lanie and Hop's son) crawl all over us.

We got into tickle wars, fake wrestling, and generally being human jungle gyms while chatting. Or the men did this. Any time one of the little ones did something that might jar me, Snap snatched them up and let them crawl all over him.

It was sweet.

It was Snap.

And seeing how amazing he was with kids was doing a number on me.

While we sat and drank and played with the boys, we talked about Joker's builds (he was young, younger than me, but he'd become *the* guy at Ride who designed and built their custom bikes and cars), Carissa's plans to become a hair stylist, and going through properties on Snap's phone that he was considering adding to his real estate empire.

It was then I learned that he didn't just buy them. He bought them, fixed them up like the one we were in, then rented them undoubtedly at high rates in order to attract a certain tenant that wouldn't give him shit or leave his places trashed and probably lined his world with cash.

He wasn't trying to be a real estate mogul.

But as I listened to him talk casually to Joker about how he handled six properties, his work at Ride, and his work with the Club, like it was nothing, not to mention looking to add to his modest but growing dynasty, he just simply was.

A biker becoming a mogul.

It was impressive.

It was attractive.

And it was surprising, but listening to him, I realized it was another side of what was all just *Snap*.

The older men kicked back on my furniture surrounding the women who were on their asses or their knees around my coffee table as they proceeded to loudly and hilariously get smashed playing a game only college students were unwise enough to play.

In that time, listening to the talk, enjoying the laughter, I did this assessing my surroundings.

And I decided on a smaller dining room table so I could have another seating area on that side of the house, definitely a reading nook so that chair could be dragged in when I had company, and a portable crib that I could keep in the garage (this last I added when Travis passed out on Joker's chest, and to my utter agony and profound delight, Nash did the same on Snap).

The women got shitfaced and loud, all but Carissa, who was surprisingly crazy-good at quarters.

Eventually their men peeled them off the floor as they declared undying love for each other, gave shit to their men for spoiling the fun, and made plans to get shitfaced again, and soon, all the while their men guided them into their coats, out the door, and then poured them in their trucks.

Except Joker and Carissa, who stayed, hanging with Mom, Snap, and me, them cuddled on one side of my couch, curled around each other providing a human crib for Travis, Mom in my armchair, and me and Snap cuddled into the other side of my couch.

Yes, I said cuddled.

I wasn't being stupid, stupid Rosalie.

I was being stupid, dreamer, happy Rosalie.

And stupid, dreamer, happy Rosalie was the "dreamer" and "happy" part of that because I saw that the night had just made my mom the "happy" part.

There was also, of course, the important addition of Snapper being a crazy-good cuddler.

Like we'd done it a million times before, with skills innate to males and females passed down from generation to generation, even if we were all together, the men talked and the women talked, holding entirely different conversations in the same space.

Mom and I learned Joker wasn't Travis's dad. He was Travis's really awesome stepdad. They lived together, had Travis every other week, Carissa worked at LeLane's, and they'd gone to high school together, been in love with each other then, but it wasn't until relatively recently they hooked up.

She gave us more and Carissa learned a lot about Mom and me.

Through this, sipping Corona, I watched her with Joker, the ease they had with each other and with Travis, and I wondered if she knew about the shit storm that was swirling around the Chaos MC.

If she did, it didn't seem to bother her in the slightest.

She had her man. She had her son. Her man loved her son and her son worshiped her man.

In the bubble of Carissa's world, all was good and happy even if the bigger bubble of the Chaos world was in danger of exploding.

Along with this I came to realize that I really liked Carissa and Joker. I liked them all. I liked that there was food and booze and fun and loudness and laughter. I liked that no one pushed Snap and Joker and me to join in, they let us be quiet in the corner with the kids. I liked that there *were* kids and they were part of what was happening in a natural way. I liked that once some folks left, we got something different, mellow and comfortable and relaxed. I liked that Snap fit into all of this like he was born to it. And I liked that Snapper fit me (and Mom) into it like we'd been there for years.

Liking all of this, lulled by all of this, eventually I passed out on Snapper's chest, still in the throes of nodding to try to stay awake as Mom and Carissa chatted.

The next thing I knew, Snap was lifting me from the couch.

"I can walk," I'd mumbled.

"That's good, baby, because you just got over a concussion and I could get you up normal stairs, but it'd be a tight fit not to slam your cranium into the center pole of these."

He put me down at the foot of the staircase and I glanced groggily around as, with Snap's hands on my hips spotting me, I lurched up the stairs.

The space was dark and empty.

"Where's Mom?" I asked.

"Joke and Carrie drove her home."

"Oh."

I made it up to the bedroom, through the bedroom and bathroom, managed to snap on the closet light and stood swaying, staring at a set of drawers in the closet.

"Where do you think my pajamas are?" I asked Snapper, who'd followed me.

He opened and closed two drawers.

And there they were in drawer number three.

I snatched up a pair that was shorts and a loose cami in a peach/mauve/lavender/gray paisley and then pulled off my tee.

That was when I sensed Snap leaving me.

I put on my pajamas, saw High had set my suitcases just inside the closet, decided I was too exhausted to dig through them for my toothbrush, and then lurched into the bedroom.

Snap was standing at the end of the bed, arms crossed on his chest, ankles crossed with boot heel up, toe down on the wood floor, watching me.

"Why aren't you in bed?" I asked.

His body jerked and his brows cocked.

"Bed," I muttered, making it to the side of that piece of furniture and yanking down the fluffy duvet.

Very fluffy.

Upon sleepy inspection, totally choice.

"Babe," Snapper called softly.

Bent over the bed, I looked to him, focused on him, saw he had not moved, and stated, "I'm stupid, dreamer, happy Rosalie right now, Snap. Please don't mess it up."

"You're not drunk," he noted.

"No," I confirmed.

"Honey—"

"Don't," I whispered.

In the dark lit generously from the huge window behind the bed, we stared into each other's eyes for long moments before he reminded me quietly, "We haven't had our conversation."

"You're messing it up," I said quietly back.

"I'm not that guy," he informed me.

"You're still messing it up," I shared.

"Help me out here, Rosie, 'cause you mean the world to me and I don't wanna do dick to fuck my chances of having a shot with you."

Okay.

God.

Just when I thought he couldn't get better.

He got better.

"Then don't leave me tonight. Because tonight has been perfect. Mom was happy. I was happy. We haven't had a perfect night since Dad got sick. The only thing that could make it not perfect is you leaving me to sleep alone. I'm not talking about anything else. Just sleeping and not doing it alone."

"All right, baby, you want that, I gotta know, the dawn comes, you aren't gonna be pissed I took advantage."

"We're gonna sleep. There won't be any advantage to take," I replied.

"Sleeping together is an intimacy, Rosie, no matter what happens, or doesn't, when you're doin' it," he informed me softly.

I loved he thought that.

God.

Better and better.

"The dawn will not bring that for you, Everett," I whispered.

It took him several very long seconds to make his decision.

He made the right one when he pulled off his thermal and let it fall to the floor.

Rather than stare at his chest and perhaps start drooling, I crawled into bed.

I watched as, drawn by moonlight, his beautiful body in gray boxer briefs got in the other side.

He settled on his back.

I scooted toward him and settled into him.

He shoved an arm under me and curled me closer.

"You okay?" I asked.

"Fuck yeah," he answered decisively.

"Maybe this isn't fair," I muttered, having second thoughts.

"Rosie, honey, you put me here, you change your mind now, you're gonna have to pry me out."

I smiled against his pec and draped my arm across his abs.

They were tight.

They felt nice.

"How much do you work out?" I asked.

"Enough."

"Enough for your average shmoe or enough for a semi-pro middleweight boxer?"

"Classed light heavyweight, Rosie."

I lifted my head and looked to his face in the moonlight.

"You box?"

"No. But I know the divisions and I'm not middleweight."

"Oh."

I saw him grin in the silver beams. "How much you work out?"

"Nine hours a shift."

He chuckled.

"No, seriously," I told him.

His fingers started drawing a pattern on my hip. "When you go back?"

"They told me to call when I'm ready. I think I'll call tomorrow."

"Ribs good enough for that?"

"I'm not supposed to do much to aggravate my torso, so I won't be carrying a tray for a while, but they said they'd put me behind the bar."

"They like you," he murmured.

"I'm likable," I teased.

His hand gripped my hip. "Yeah, you are."

I settled again into his pec.

"Those ribs, baby, you should sleep on your back," he noted.

"I'm here, you're gonna have to pry me away."

His body shook gently with his humor but his arm around me got tighter.

It felt sweet.

"These mattresses are super-comfortable," I remarked.

"Rosie?" he called.

"Yeah," I answered.

"You were dead to the world and barely able to maneuver the stairs ten minutes ago."

"Is that biker speak for you're tired and want me to shut up?" I asked.

"Pretty much," he told me.

I smiled against his pec.

We both fell silent and it was Snap that broke it.

He did it careful. He did it gentle.

He did it Snap.

"You scared of bein' alone, honey?" he asked.

Man, it was crazy how well he knew me.

"A little," I whispered.

He gently rolled me toward him so I was more full-frontal against his side, murmuring, "I got you."

I closed my eyes tight.

I had not been "got" in a really long time.

I did not want to be one of those women who could not do without a man.

But I feared I was one of those women who couldn't do without a man.

Or, alternately, I lost the man who had me my whole life, and like Mom said, I'd gone reeling. And at the time when I was ready to attempt to stand on my own two feet, God had thrown into my path the man who was perfect for me.

But I was on a long, ugly roll of losing men that meant something to me. I'd barely survived the most important one.

What would happen if I lost the only one on this earth who was perfect for me?

"It's all gonna be good, Rosie," he said.

I really wished I could believe he was right.

"Okay, Snapper."

"Go to sleep," he ordered.

"All right, honey."

He drew in a deep breath and let it go.

I kept my eyes closed (I just didn't do that tight).

It didn't take long before I fell asleep.

The pain in my ribs drove me to my back in the middle of the night.

But now, here I was again, tucked to Snapper's side with his hand resting on my hip.

"Awake?" Snap asked, his deep voice thick with sleep.

"It's past dawn," I told him.

"Yeah," he agreed.

"And right now I'd totally kiss you if I'd grabbed my toothbrush last night and wasn't terrified of morning breath," I declared.

I just got out the word "breath" before I found myself hauled full on top of Snapper's long, lean body and I was looking in Snapper's downy-snowy-sleepy eyes.

"I don't give a fuck about morning breath," he growled.

So be it.

I tilted my head.

And I kissed him.

Now this…

This…

This was the *perfect* first kiss.

Both our mouths were open before our lips touched and both our tongues were out and tangling before our lips settled.

I didn't know about me but he tasted wet and warm and musky and I barely had that taste before I wanted more.

So I tilted my head further and gave Snap more in order to get *my* more.

I knew he wanted it because he didn't hesitate to take it.

He also gave it, keeping one arm wrapped firm around my waist, the other hand trailed up my back, twining in my hair to hold me to his mouth.

It lasted long and it went deep and every millisecond was a thing of pure beauty before he gently fisted his fingers in my hair, tugged back a bit, and pulled his mouth from mine.

"That was fuckin' spectacular, Rosie, but I gotta ask you to help me out again," he rumbled.

I'd help him any way he wanted.

"What?" I breathed.

He shifted me on his body so "what" was without a doubt digging with steely determination into the flesh of my belly.

And "what" felt *heavenly*.

"Gonna get up and grab a shower, yeah?" he said. "You snooze. I'll make you breakfast then I gotta go."

Wait.

He was going to...

What?

"Snapper—"

"I want that," he all but snarled, his eyes suddenly flooded with heat, which sent a reciprocal wave of the same blazing through me.

Unfortunately (but also amazingly), he kept talking.

"But we're doin' this right, Rosie. We're talkin' and we're gettin' shit straight because we're not just doin' this right, I'm doin' *you* right. For years, you've had a rough ride, what's happened recently just the most recent. You've been jacked around since your daddy died and I don't think either man meant to do you wrong but in the end they did. And I'm the man who's gonna do you right, Rosalie. With me, that rough ride is gonna end, baby. So as much as I want more of what you're offering, I'll take it tonight when we both know where we're at and I can be assured you're right there with me."

Perfect for me.

I stared into his eyes as I slid my hand up his chest, his neck, into the bristles on his cheek.

Holding him there, holding his gaze, only then did I whisper, "Thank you for being you, Snap."

He made a noise that sounded in my womb before he rolled, his rock-solid cock now pressed to my hip, his chest looming over me for a scant second before he laid another wet, hot, crazy-awesome one on me and then lifted his head to me panting and holding on to his shoulders.

"Stop bein' you for five seconds so I can get outta this bed," he ordered gruffly.

Snapper sounded nice talking gruffly.

But I nearly burst out laughing, contained it and beat back the snort doing that welled up in me before I asked, "Who do you want me to be?"

"Someone annoying."

"Snapper," I whined dramatically, "you know I don't like it when you throw your clothes on the floor."

"Now you're bein' cute and I still wanna fuck you."

"I have syphilis," I lied.

He started laughing.

"And I used to be a man," I went on.

He started laughing harder.

"A gay man, so we're good," I told him.

He laughed even harder.

I slid my hands from his shoulders up to cup his jaw and said quietly, "I hate to end this goodness because you laughing is a beautiful thing but I need you to take a shower, have breakfast, and leave me by myself, because except in my car, I haven't been alone since it happened and I've gotta learn to do that again, hopefully without freaking."

The laughter vanished and he dipped his face close to me.

"I'll show you how to use the alarm before I go," he said.

I nodded.

"And whatever I do today, I'll do it close so if you get too freaked, you call me and I can be here fast."

"Don't change your—"

"Rosie, that's just the way it's gonna be today and every day until you're feelin' good about things."

Perfect for me.

I nodded again.

"And I'll be back tonight around six. I'll bring dinner. What do you want?" he asked.

"What are my choices?"

"Any place that does takeaway in the Denver Metro Area."

"That's an alarming amount of choice, Snapper Kavanaugh."

"It's what you got, Rosalie Holloway."

"Narrow it down for me, Mulder," I ordered and the instant I did, the look in his eyes…

Man.

I'd leap through rings of fire to give him that look again.

He liked we had that. Him my Mulder, me his Scully. He liked getting it back. He liked that familiarity. That history. That sweetness we shared, him and me.

Perfect for me.

"Indian or Mexican," he said softly.

"Indian."

"You got a favorite?" he asked.

"Butter chicken," I told him.

"Noted," he said.

"Or chicken tikka masala," I shared.

"Right."

"Or chicken korma," I said.

"Rosie—"

"Or shrimp biryani. And onion bhaji, mushroom bhaji, tikka skewers, samosas. Anything with paneer in it. I also like keema. And don't forget the pilau rice, naan and papadums."

I shut up.

Snap stared at me.

I continued to be silent.

"You done?" he asked.

"Aloo gobi," I said quietly.

He busted out laughing.

He gave me a quick kiss on the lips still doing it, and continuing to do it, he pulled away and asked, "What do you want me to make you for breakfast?"

"LaMar's," I shared.

He shook his head, still laughing, and also asking, "You got one or two choices to give me or do I gotta get through another recitation?"

"Buttermilk glazed or Bavarian cream."

"Gotcha," he said, gave me another quick kiss, then rolled away.

I watched his ass as he got out of bed and I watched a lot of things as he walked around the end of it to the bathroom, all of them *awesome*.

Then I lay on my new mattresses (that Snapper gave me) and looked to the ceiling of my bedroom in my new house (that Snapper gave me).

And I thought, *What the hell am I doing?*

I knew.

But I didn't know.

I knew it was right.

And I was terrified it was wrong.

I wanted to grab hold to all that had been given to me (and my mom) from the instant we walked into this carriage house.

And I felt fear tearing into me that if I did, I'd finally have it all again.

Which meant having everything to lose…

Again.

Chapter Six

Beautiful

Rosalie

I stood in bra and panties, leaning over the basin in my new bathroom, staring at my face in the mirror.

The bruising down either side of my inner eyes was now just shadows. Except for the pad prints of Beck's fingers, all the discoloration on my neck was gone. Sometime since yesterday, the final stitches had fallen out of the gash in my brow and the one on my jaw, leaving only red marks I hoped would recede. And the tape was coming off my nose tomorrow at my final follow-up with my doctor.

Lifting my chin so I could see them both, I stared at the red marks.

Rainman had opened up my brow. When it happened, I felt it tearing. He always wore heavy rings and made it clear in heinous ways that he felt like continuing to be accessorized during the festivities.

Those rings had skulls on them.

And some had crosses.

So he'd opened me up with what amounted to a crucifix, marking me maybe forever, reminding me every time I looked at myself or someone's eyes drifted that way of my time spent in that warehouse.

Every time any brother of Chaos looked at me, they'd be reminded too.

And most of all, Snapper would too.

I lifted my hands, rubbed them through the wet hair I'd combed back after my shower and moved to the closet, doing an inventory and finding out where all my stuff was.

I tugged on jeans, went back to the bathroom, sprayed on deodorant and perfume, then back to the drawers in the closet to grab a cream cami-shell. I pulled it on, then snatched out a thin, nearly see-through, dusky-blue, five-button thermal that didn't even pretend to be about keeping me warm.

The buttons undone (like they were then, like I always wore them) showed some cleavage. The material clearly displayed the shell. It was a full torso, subtly sexy peek-a-boo worn by a scarred, beaten, disposed-of biker old lady.

"Okay, damn, where is my head at today?" I snapped, forcing myself to pull it together.

I had to call Colombo's and tell them I was good to go on the next schedule. I had to unpack the bags that were filled with stuff Mom had run to my old place to grab while I was in the hospital because we both knew I wouldn't be going back there until I could face it before we knew I wasn't going to go back there at all. I needed to familiarize myself with where the Chaos old ladies had put my stuff and move anything if they'd done it the way I didn't want it.

And I needed to think about what I wanted to get out of the conversation that night with Snapper because I'd let stupid, dreamer, happy Rosalie get the better of me last night and I'd used him to cuddle with and sleep with and make myself feel safe.

But now I needed to decide where my head was at because he didn't deserve me playing with his heart.

I went to the bedroom, made the bed, padded down the stairs and inspected the kitchen, doing the minimal cleanup of the donuts Snap and I had dragged on last night's clothes and went out to get, that we'd brought back and eaten standing up at the counter before he took off. This being crunching up the donut bag and tossing it into the built-in trash drawer.

I poured myself another cup of coffee and sipped at it, opening and closing cupboards, finding the women had done me right in more ways than I already knew. They set me up perfectly.

I took the coffee with me as I wandered and found, through the other door on the wall down from the powder room, there was a nicely outfitted laundry room with washer and dryer, soaking sink, shelves and wall-mounted dryer racks.

I mean, seriously.

I could live here the rest of my life and be happy.

Though it wouldn't fit any Travises or Nashes.

Or Hermiones.

Just me.

A man and me.

I heard my phone ring and I moved out of the laundry room to the table by the door where it was sitting, deciding next up was the goodness I knew I'd discover digging through the Sephora bag that was still there.

I set my coffee down and picked up my phone.

The screen said *Snap* and seeing it my heart felt happy that he could finally be displayed on my phone for anyone to see that he was in my life and thus belonged in my phone.

But my head felt full of ominous gray clouds.

"Hey," I greeted after I took the call.

"Hey to you," he replied. "You good?"

I closed my eyes, opened them, and stared at the long stretch of lawn that led to the street.

There were bushes down either side of the property. I couldn't begin to know what they were, just that they were cut low for the winter.

I wondered if Snap provided lawn maintenance for his tenants, and if he did, if he did that himself or if he expected them to do it as part of the rental agreement.

"Rosalie," he called, his tone sharper.

Not sharper.

Worried.

"I'm good," I told him, though I wasn't sure I was considering how it felt that he'd been gone maybe a little over an hour and he was already calling me, checking on me.

That should feel good.

It was just my head was so messed up, I wouldn't let it.

"You don't sound good," he noted.

"The stitches all fell out," I shared.

"Noticed," he murmured.

Of course he had.

"I'm gonna have scars," I told him.

There was a beat of silence before he declared, "I'm comin' back."

"Snap, don't."

"Babe, you went from bein' cute in bed and smiling eating a donut to whatever the fuck you sound like now and talking about scars. You've fallen into your head, it's not a good place to be, so I'm comin' back."

"I need to sort this stuff out for myself, Snapper."

"Why?" he asked.

Suddenly, the big yard in front of me was blurry.

"Sorry?" I asked back.

"Why do you have to do it yourself?"

I...

Didn't know.

I told him what I did know.

"I've relied on a man all my life, Snap."

"Okay, so?"

My head jerked.

"That's not very strong," I pointed out.

"Have I ever told you why I joined Chaos?" he queried.

I felt my shoulders straighten because he hadn't, I knew something big was coming, and last, I bucked up so I could be prepared because I wanted so badly to know that something big.

Precisely...why he'd joined Chaos.

"No," I told him.

"I'm a quiet guy. I've always been that guy. First thing I did when I got my driver's license was go to a movie by myself," he shared.

There was something immensely cool about that.

There was also something immensely Snapper about that.

Then again, it was kinda one and the same thing.

"Was the first I did that," he went on. "Wasn't the last. My brother and sister, they got big personalities. They're almost pathologically social. Just like my mom and dad. My sister, she's crazy. Lovable, but crazy. Always getting into trouble. Fightin' with Mom. Then lovin' on her. My brother was the big man, sports star. Soccer. Really good at it. Earned a scholarship on it. I played tennis."

I felt a sudden, inappropriate-at-that-juncture giggle welling up in me and choked it back.

But I couldn't quite hide the disbelief in my, "You played *tennis*?"

"That's all about me. The court. The racket. The ball. My game. My strategy. It isn't even about my opponent. He was just someone who, if he could, lobbed the ball back at me, and it was up to me to get a bead on his strategy. You are totally in your own space. You are totally in your own head. Win or lose, it's all on you."

I could see this about Snap and not just the fact that, knowing this, I realized he had a tennis player's body, if that tennis player was Boris Becker.

"I read," he continued. "I ride. I don't play tennis anymore and haven't since high school but when I did, I liked it. I got my properties and those are mine. I buy them. I manage them. Brothers might help out fixin' them up, but the vision and the follow-through is all on me."

"Okay," I said when he stopped talking.

"But back then, whatever I got into doing, I went home to my family. I was the middle kid but I didn't get any of that middle kid mindfuck bullshit because they were the way they were. Totally not like me but they didn't make me feel like an outsider because I was how I was. They gave me space to be me. They came to my matches. I went to their shit. I didn't exist among them. I was part of them as who I was, not how they wished I would be. That's still my place. They get together a lot more than I get with them, but when I show, I'm just as much a part of my family as the rest of them. It's just that I'm not into family game night every two weeks and they don't give a shit I'm not. They're happy for me to show when I want to show. They take me when I want to give them time and they leave me be when I'm not feelin' it."

"That's cool," I said when he paused.

"I wanted more of that," he shared. "I wanted to be around people who let me be me. I didn't want to be in a corporate situation where it was about toeing the line or clawing to the top. I didn't want to be in a different situation where every day was the same until you realized your life was a long line of drudgery. I wanted a family but I wanted that with freedom."

"That makes sense," I noted.

"And since I ride, since my bike is a big part of my life, since that freedom is the biggest part of me, I found a brotherhood that shared the same ideals. And the biggest part of those ideals, I give it to them and they give it to me. That 'it' being, I let the brothers be the brothers and all the brothers let me be me."

"I love that you found that, Snapper," I said softly.

"I do too, Rosie," he returned. "And the point I'm makin' with that is, if I wanna hole up in my room in the Compound and read a book, I can. Then I can walk right out and share a beer with a brother. I can be alone, but I'm never alone. Are you with me?"

I was with him.

And I was breathing funny.

"Babe, are you with me?" he pushed when I said nothing.

"I'm with you, honey," I forced out.

"I got somethin' on my mind, I go to Tack. I go to High. I go to Hop or Pete. Or I go to my dad or my brother. I don't wanna ride alone, Joke goes out with me. Or Boz. Or Hound. I can put in a kitchen but that's not my thing, how it should look, so if I need to buy a sink that works for one of my places, Tyra helps me. Or my sister helps me. Or my mom tells me what she thinks would work."

"That's all important, but what I'm saying about me at this point in my life is different than all that," I told him carefully.

"You think if my mom died or something ugly happened to my sister that those brothers and their women wouldn't be all about being there for me?" he asked.

I looked at my toes.

"Rosalie," he growled.

"They would," I whispered.

"It isn't about havin' someone to share a beer with, even when it is. It isn't about havin' someone to do a ride with, even when it's that too. It's about making the conscious decision to surround myself with good people so when life is good, I got someone to share that with, and when life turns to shit, I got someone who'll help hold me steady."

Now I was deep breathing.

"Life, Rosie," he said gently, "is not about goin' it alone. It's about finding the right people to share it with who will make it better when it's good and be there to hold you steady when it's not."

"But I'm bouncing from guy to guy to guy," I pointed out.

"You're living your life and you aren't doin' it latchin' on to men to take care of you. You're doin' it and men are drifting through your life while that's happening. They weren't the right ones and right now, that's good for me, because I wanna be that one. But they aren't anything except that they *were*. They *were* in your life. And you moved on or they moved on or whatever. You wanna be with somebody, that does not make you weak, Rosie. In most cases, finding it in you to take the risk to trust your time and your heart to someone makes you strong. But in all cases, wanting to share your life with other people just makes you human."

"You've got it totally figured out," I muttered.

"No, Rosie, I got dick figured out," he retorted. "Only thing I know for certain is, so far, I lucked out and made good decisions in my life, and one of them is you. The you that it doesn't mean shit you got a scar cuttin' 'cross your brow like it wouldn't mean shit you put on fifty pounds like it wouldn't mean shit you aged thirty years. You're Rosie. And no matter what, you'll always be beautiful."

My throat sounded clogged when I pushed through it, "I don't think you need to come back anymore, Snapper."

"You don't sound much better, baby," he said softly.

"Then you aren't listening very closely."

He grew silent.

I stared at my toes fighting against crying.

He broke the silence.

"Now, tell me what you got planned for your day."

I cleared my throat, lifted my gaze, and focused on his tidy, winter yard. "Unpacking. Calling Colombo's. Online shopping to build a vision for my reading nook."

Your reading nook.

Damn.

"That all sounds good but not sure it's gonna fill up your day, Rosie."

He wanted me to fill up my day so I had good things to do, things to stay busy with, things that would keep me from getting in my head and messing with my own damn self.

And that was so damn *Snapper.*

"I also need rugs, a dining room table, garden furniture, another seating area," *and a portable crib.* I didn't share the last. I didn't want him freaking at this point. One of us freaking was enough. I just finished, "I think now that I'm feeling better, I'm going to consider the rest of the time off more of a vacation and relax. Check in with Mom. Just…be."

"That sounds like it'll work," he murmured.

I drew in a deep breath.

"You fall back into your head and it isn't good, Rosie, you call me," he ordered.

"Okay, Snapper."

"I'll text when I'm on my way tonight with food."

"Okay."

"Right, I'll let you go now."

"Uh...Snap?"

"Right here."

I drew in another deep breath then said, "Thanks, honey, for pulling me out of my head."

"Thanks for letting me."

That had me closing my eyes again, dropping my head and opening them to stare at my toes.

"Pedicure," I mumbled.

"Say again?"

"I'm going to give myself a pedicure today."

"Call your mom and go out and get one with her."

"That sounds perfect."

It did and I decided to set that up before I even called Colombo's.

And Snap sounded like he was smiling when he replied, "Great. Later, Scully."

"The truth is out there, Mulder. It's also in here, since you just laid a ton of it on me."

The last thing I heard before he disconnected was him chuckling.

I loved that.

So much I memorized that in a way I hoped to God I'd never forget that moment and the sound of Snapper's humor after all he'd just given me.

Then I took my phone from my ear and called my mother.

* * * *

"Okay, give it to me, what's going on with my Rosalie," Mom ordered.

I'd unpacked. Colombo's knew to put me on rotation. We'd had lunch, then manis and pedis. Now we were sitting on the couch in front of the windows at Fortnum's Used Bookstore having a latte as crafted by a crazy man who looked like serial killers never looked, but you expected them to, who made the absolute best coffee in Denver.

And I was not surprised that my mom had read me.

"Snapper is coming over for dinner tonight and to have a heavy conversation about what's next for him and me," I shared.

"Good. And after that takes five minutes to figure out, I hope he gives you an orgasm during your first time which would round him out as utterly perfect for you," she shot back.

I stared at her.

"Your father would love him," she declared, leaned into me, and repeated with emphasis, "*Love him.*"

He absolutely would.

And that felt crazy-good.

It was high time I laid it out.

And as ever, I laid it out with my mother.

"Mom, Chaos is at war with a man called Benito Valenzuela. He's the head of a syndicate that sells drugs, runs guns, peddles flesh, and makes porno movies."

I watched my mom's mouth turn down.

"And Chaos are vigilantes," I kept going. "Even before this war with this Benito guy cropped up, they patrolled their turf and if they found something happening they didn't like, this being illegal activities, they didn't...and still don't...call the police." I paused, studied her closely and asked, "Are you understanding me?"

"I...uh, is this a bad thing?" she asked back.

Seriously?

I leaned toward her and hissed, "*Mom!* Snapper and his brothers are at war and they act like Chaos turf is Tombstone, they're the Earp brothers, and they have every right to police it when it's *not* Tombstone. It's Denver. Well, parts are Englewood," I meandered off target and then got back to it. "And Denver, *and* Englewood, have their own police."

"So they're an outlaw biker club who are outlaws by being citizens that make people obey the law," she said.

That sounded almost...

Noble.

Damn.

"Well...yeah," I replied.

"And this is bad because...?" she asked.

"Because it's dangerous," I snapped.

"And did you know this happened when you dated that Shy person?" she inquired.

"Not really, that's when I found out," I told her.

"And you didn't end things with him when he turned out to be a vigilante?" she pushed.

I shut up.

She still knew my answer since I didn't end things with Shy. He'd ended them with me.

Thus she kept talking.

"And, although you didn't share the fullness of your maneuvers with Chaos against Bounty with your mother, you put your behind on the line for Chaos against your old man's club knowing they had something planned for your old man's club. And since that is not about Chaos turf in Denver or Englewood, but things happening on Bounty turf in Aurora, this had something to do with this war with this Benito person you also knew about."

"I heard Beck talking about what his brothers were getting into. And that Benito guy. And the Chaos situation. And old ladies and biker groupies chat. So, not all of it, but yeah, I knew enough of it."

"Enough of it you approached Chaos to help out," she surmised.

I shut up again.

"Because you wanted Beck to sort himself out," she kept at me.

"At first," I said.

"And when he continued to go along with his club when they were doing seriously stupid stuff that put you all in danger, you gave up on him and started to see what else was out there, even if this happened unintentionally. That something else in your face and your life and involved with this situation," she deduced.

I nodded.

She nodded back and kept going.

"I think it's important to note that you were in danger even before you informed on your old man's club, Rosalie. The authorities don't like anyone enjoying ill-gotten gains, not even those who gained them consequently. This might not mean you'd be prosecuted when they'd gotten caught. What it would mean is that, if you'd bought a home with Beck's dirty money, it would be taken from you. If you'd bought a car, it would be taken from you. If you'd had children with him, the powers that be might concern themselves with your ability to make good choices for yourself and your children, and they might consider taking them from you. And Beck made conscious decisions to put you right there. It was *you* who made conscious decisions to get you and him *out*."

"I know what happened, Mom," I said carefully.

"And in the meantime, you met Snapper, who came to mean something to you, something deep and good and important. A Snapper who is with a club at war with a man who *peddles flesh* and *makes porn* and your issue is…?" she prompted.

"He might get hurt," I told her.

"Yes, and a police officer faces every shift every day with that same risk."

And finally we were where I needed us to be.

"Snap is not police," I pointed out.

"And a soldier faces that every day when they're deployed," she kept on like I didn't say anything.

"He's not a soldier either, Mom."

She jerked her head to the side. "He isn't?"

I shut up again.

"You know," she carried on, "in a perfect world, there are rules and everyone abides by them. There is good and there is bad and everyone understands which is which. There is dark and there is light and each person understands which they carry inside them. But this isn't a perfect world, Rosalie, and it never will be. In every case, in every instance, in every nook and cranny on this planet, the lines are blurred. Each person has to decide their version of what is right and what is *not*. And so far, you haven't told me anything that, according to my version, isn't right about Snapper Kavanaugh or his Club."

"I'm scared of losing him to this war," I told her.

"And he's deeply in love with you. How do you think he's felt all these months you've been a part of an outlaw motorcycle club you've been informing on, Rosalie? How well do you think he's slept knowing he couldn't protect you every second of every day? And now, when what happened to you happened, living with how that might scar you and he's powerless over that too."

Not exactly.

He was so far really good at handling that last part.

That said, I'd never considered how Snapper might have felt about what danger I was putting myself in. I'd just pushed him away when worse came to worse and he was blaming himself and hurting for me and wanting to step up to take care of me.

Not wanting to do it.

Doing it.

God!

Now I not only had a messed-up head, I was a selfish bitch.

"Life is a risk, Rosalie," she said impatiently, cutting into my thoughts. "And I totally understand you being hesitant after that pack of mongrels set themselves on you. But I hope I raised a daughter stronger than that. A daughter who can get herself past that and recognize what's good for her, grab hold, and keep it close and safe for as long as God gives her the privilege of having it."

I looked away and sipped coffee, right then worried that I wasn't that daughter she'd hoped she'd raised.

The coffee was awesome, and as such fortifying, but nothing could be fortifying enough to pull my stuff together on this.

Mom's tone was a lot gentler when she noted, "You say you're in love with him."

"I fell in love with him while I was with another man," I told the nicked coffee table covered in spent magazines and used books for sale that had been taken from shelves, perused over coffee, and left for next time.

"Honeypot," she called.

I looked to her.

"Do you feel guilt for not being loyal in your heart to Beck?" she asked.

"Yes," I answered tightly. "And Mom," I went on when her face started to set hard, "it isn't all about Beck, even if part of it is. It's about wondering what Snap will think that I could do that to Beck when he might be up next."

Understanding dawned on her. "Ah."

"Yeah," I mumbled. "Ah."

"So, along with healing after being gang-beaten, moved into a new space, worried what your ex's club has planned for you, and concerned about the activities of the man you're currently in love with, you're also bearing the burden that if you try it with him, the way it started between you, he'll never truly trust you."

There was absolutely all that.

There was also the scar thing, but Snapper took care of that.

Gah!

"Yes," I answered Mom.

"And what does Snapper say about all of this?"

"I think this is going to be our conversation tonight."

All of a sudden, she leaned into me, latched her fingers around my forearm and whispered fiercely, "Be the daughter I raised and recognize what's good for you, fucking *grab hold*, keep it close, and keep it *precious*, Rosalie, for as long as God gives you the privilege of having it."

I stared at my mom with big eyes.

My father was a swearer. He could be working on something in the garage that wasn't going right and let out a string of swear words that lasted five whole minutes that would make a sailor raise his brows.

My mother hardly ever swore.

So the f-word was huge.

But what she was urging me to do was even more huge.

"You like him," I whispered.

She let me go, sat back, and said exasperatedly, "Oh for goodness sakes, Rosalie. *Obviously*. I mean, what's not to like?" Then she sucked back an irate sip of her coffee, tasted it, and the irritation fled as the miracle of a serial-killer-but-not-serial-killer-looking barista's artistry touched her taste buds.

"Mom?" I called.

She turned her eyes to me.

My eyes to me.

I loved my eyes. I loved my mother.

But I wished I got just a little piece of my dad.

"I miss Dad," I admitted.

She leaned back toward me, her face melting into sheer beauty.

"Of course you do, sweetie. He was the kind of man who was always going to leave a huge hole in the world of those he loved when he left them. The kind of hole, honeypot," she leaned even closer, "that feels when he's gone like it'll *never* get filled. Don't try to fill it, Rosalie. Let it sit because it's not empty. It's filled to bursting with the love he had for you and the memories he gave our family. It isn't the same as having him. It never will be. But it's a treasure regardless. So learn to treasure it and do what he'd want you to do. Find someone to love you, to make new treasured memories with. And don't let fears and loss hold you back. That isn't the daughter I raised. But more, that isn't the daughter your father raised."

I stared at her, muttering, "Oh no, I'm going to start crying."

"Okay, I have Kleenex," she replied.

"Mom!" I exclaimed kinda loudly. "I don't want to start crying."

She looked perplexed. "Why in the world not?"

"Because…because…because…" I didn't know why. "Because I'm seeing Snapper later. It'll mess up my makeup and make my eyes all puffy."

She waved her hand in front of her face, took another sip of coffee, got a fleeting look reminiscent of what she looked like after Dad was done with her, then said, "That's why God made washcloths and Visine. Cold compresses take the puffy away and Visine rids the red. Walgreens is just down the street. If you don't have Visine, we'll get you some drops before you head home. And some condoms. I'm sure with the man Snapper is, he'll come prepared, but just in case."

I stopped wanting to cry and started smiling.

"Do you know how much I love you?" I asked.

She looked me right in the eye and answered, "Yes."

Damn.

I felt like crying again.

Instead of crying, I jumped and looked up when the huge, serial-killer-looking-not-a-serial-killer, wild-gray-and-blond-haired, crazy-russet-bearded barista smashed two coffee mugs on the table before us and boomed, "Jesus Jones! I don't even know what you bitches are talking about and you're killin' my mood. Suck more of that back and get over this shit. I got a new litter of kitties that came in last night I get to go home and play with. I don't wanna be on a downer when I got new kitties."

Mom and I stared up at him, agog, and I was pretty sure both of us didn't know which part of his boom to be most agog about.

He retreated behind the coffee machine as the beautiful redheaded lady who owned the place took up the space he'd exited.

"Sorry about Tex calling you bitches, bossing you around, and freaking you out talking about kittens. He's kind of a cat lover. And a crazy guy. The, uh…coffees are on the house." She then took off on a stomp and did it shouting toward the coffee machine, "Tex, swear to

God, the next customers you—"

"Zip it, sister!" the crazy man called Tex interrupted her on a bellow. "You're not stealin' my new kitty thunder with your attitude either!"

"I'm not stealing your new kitty thunder!" she shouted back. "I'm trying to retain customers so I can buy that new pair of cowboy boots Lee says I can't have because I already have fifteen pairs."

"Like you're hurtin'. This store turns over a shitload and your husband's rollin' in it," Tex retorted.

"And like she cares Lee says she can't have them," Mom and I heard whispered from our sides, this coming from a pretty blonde lady who had a smile that made her a knockout. "She already bought those boots. She just wants Tex to pipe down and not freak people out."

Mom and I looked in unison to the silent standoff Tex and the redhead were having with their eyes, but we looked back to the blonde when she spoke again.

"And it isn't about his mood," she said. "He's worried about your bandage. It doesn't look like it, but he's a ladies' man in the good kind of way, really protective, and he doesn't like what he sees. He doesn't know you but he does know people like his coffee, and since that's all he can give, he gave it. So really, he's just a big, crazy, kinda scary softie."

She delivered that, then she swiped up a used mug that had been there when we sat there and took off.

"Don't ya just love this place?" we heard from the table in the corner that was on the other side of us and our heads swung that way. "These people are freakin' *loco*," the woman there went on. "You never know the shenanigans they'll get up to. Honestly, and I know this'll say it all, I don't actually come here for the coffee. That's just the icing on the cake. I come here for the floorshow. It never disappoints."

She lifted her foamy-topped latte our way and turned back to the book she was not-so-much reading.

I looked to Mom.

Her eyes drifted to me.

And then we burst out laughing.

In the midst of it, we heard boomed, "See! Look at those bitches now, Indy Nightingale! My work is done!"

So of course we laughed harder.

Chapter Seven

World

Rosalie

I was kinda embarrassed that I essentially watched out the window, waiting for Snapper since around five minutes after he texted to say he'd picked up the food and was on his way.

And when he arrived, still watching, I was totally shocked when he got out of his truck and went around to the passenger side to nab two plastic bags stuffed with stacked food containers.

There had to be enough food in those to feed six people.

I didn't know what he'd read (and was beyond caring) when I opened the front door way before he got close to it. Snapper probably already caught me watching through the window (I'd be hard to miss) so it didn't matter anyway.

But really, I was just glad he was there and I didn't care he knew it.

"You should have parked in the garage, Mulder," I told him when he was six feet away.

"I don't have a remote, Scully," he replied.

"You don't have a remote to your own garage?" I asked.

He made it to me and I stepped aside for him and his two bags to get through.

And he did this saying, "It's your garage, Rosie."

"I don't even have a rental agreement."

Snap had no reply to that.

He just walked to the kitchen.

I closed the door and followed him, asking, "Is the whole Club coming over for dinner?"

He dumped the bags on the countertop, turned, shrugging off his cut to toss it also on the counter, revealing a skintight cream thermal that was drool-worthy, and grinned at me. "I wanted you to have what you wanted so I bought everything you said you liked, but before you get grateful on me, I had an ulterior motive since Indian leftovers are the shit."

I loved the first part of that and he was right about the second part, so I smiled back.

He started undoing the tied handles of the bags while I decided not to get stuck on the fact that it was a hair down day for Snapper, and I liked it, as well as the fact that he was letting his beard grow in, though it was still longer at the chin, and the way the growth was progressing looked crazy-good on him.

Instead, I tore my eyes away from his unique brand of handsomeness and got out plates, cutlery, and beers.

"You have a good time with your mom?" he asked, taking out the containers, lining them up on the counter and flipping them open.

"We always have a good time," I answered.

"She's pretty awesome," he murmured.

She was.

I was just thrilled to know he thought she was.

"She likes you too," I shared.

His head turned my way and the expression on his face told me this sounded like a throwaway conversation, but it was anything but to Snapper. He wanted my mom to like him because he wanted a future with me.

"Good," he said.

I tucked my hair behind my ear and grabbed some spoons, shoving them in the containers as Snap opened them.

We dished up, grabbed our beers, and headed to my couch. I settled in, ready to tuck in, feeling nervous and shy.

This wasn't about the conversation we were going to have. Snap hadn't left much in doubt that he wanted to go there with me. We had some tough stuff to get through, but Snapper had proved he was adept at handling me.

It was about after, when we'd go another *there*.

It was all well and good waking up with Snapper mostly naked in the bed he bought me in the house he'd given me after a perfect night.

But right then it was so much more.

If this conversation went well, this was going to happen.

And I knew it meant everything to him.

It meant the same to me.

So that other there we might be going to tonight had to go *awesome*.

Snap didn't join me on the couch at first.

Instead, he put his plate and beer down on the coffee table and moved to the fireplace. He turned a knob on the side and the fire jumped to life.

He didn't whip out his phone and set the speakers I'd noticed that were set in the ceiling to playing Marvin Gaye's "Let's Get It On."

But it still set the scene.

Oh yeah.

I was nervous and feeling shy.

I pushed some butter chicken into the center pile of rice and shoved it in my mouth.

Snap sat opposite me on the couch and grabbed his plate.

I chewed, swallowed, and asked, "Do you do the yard work?"

He looked to me. "Come again?"

"The yard." I jerked my head toward the door behind us. "It's all set for the winter. Do you do the yard work?"

"No," he told me.

He didn't expound.

Then again, he didn't really need to.

I looked to the plate, shoved some chicken korma into the rice and ate that, still staring at my plate.

"What gives, Scully?" he asked.

I looked to him, chewed, swallowed and said, "Nothing gives."

His eyes narrowed. "You're bein' weird."

"I am?" I asked.

But I was.

I was all the way across the couch, shoved into a corner, my plate in front of my chin like I hadn't had food in six months and was intent to shovel it in, my body screaming, "This is my space, do not invade it!"

"We're eating and having a conversation. I'm not gonna jump you on the couch through butter chicken," he stated.

"You turned on the fire," I pointed out.

"So? That fire rocks. It's February. It was a pain in the ass to get that fucker in and I've never had the opportunity to enjoy it. So I turned it on."

"It's romantic," I said softly.

"Yeah," he agreed. "I'm here. You're here. We're gonna sort our shit so I'm feelin' romantic, baby. But I'm hungry and we got shit to talk about so before I do anything about that feeling, I'm gonna eat and we're gonna talk, and if we're both there after, we'll explore that feeling. Right now, it's just nice to be sitting on a couch, just you and me, having dinner. We've never had that. So might as well do it up right."

He did that all the time.

He always did it up right.

And he was very correct.

It was nice to be there, just Snap and me, for the first time.

It just sucked there was so much heavy we had to get through, hopefully successfully, before we could get past it.

I decided right then it was time to get past it.

"You know, you mean the world to me too," I blurted.

He blinked.

I kept blurting.

"It's just that I'm worried about losing you to whatever is going on with Benito Valenzuela and Bounty, because I'm guessing that's dangerous. And I know Chaos are vigilantes and you patrol your turf and that makes me anxious. I also was with a guy but then started falling for you when I was with that guy and obviously you know I was with that guy so now you know that happened, and I'm worried that you're gonna think I'm messed up, going from guy to guy to guy even when I'm *with* a guy and that might happen to you. The part, I mean, about jumping to another guy when I'm with you."

I took in a huge breath and then kept talking.

"This house is beautiful and the bed is amazing but we haven't talked about how much rent is gonna be so you're not out money, looking after me. We also haven't talked about how I'm gonna pay you back for the bed. And Mom pointed something out today that I feel crap about, knowing you had feelings for me and I was doing something dangerous, which probably worried you sick since you couldn't protect me. And this makes me think that I'm all about me, or that you'll think I'm all about me. Selfish and self-involved and not considering other people's feelings."

When I stopped talking and kept silent for a while, Snapper spoke.

"Is that it?"

He wanted more?

"Isn't that enough?" I queried.

He nodded and said, "Just makin' sure that's all we got."

"Um...do *you* have anything you wanna discuss?" I asked and finished apprehensively. "I mean, since it seems we're setting the night's agenda."

He looked like he was trying hard not to start laughing.

Then his white teeth came out, sunk right in the center of his beautiful lower lip just like they did at Zip's. I got mesmerized at the same time sidetracked, and it was me wondering if I should jump him through the butter chicken.

Sadly, he let his lip go and spoke, breaking the spell.

"How about we break yours down first?" he suggested.

I didn't know whether to be happy we weren't going to push any weird small talk and instead were going to get it out of the way or to be freaked that what he said intimated that he had items for the agenda.

I didn't comment on this. I just nodded.

He swallowed the load of Indian food he'd put in his mouth waiting for me to nod, reached out and nabbed his beer, took a swig, then set it aside and turned back to me.

Then he started.

"Valenzuela and Bounty, Rosalie, they are not your problem."

He said this unyielding, like he could just get away with saying that and I'd let that go when we were talking about *really bad* bad guys and a beef with a rival motorcycle club, not to mention vigilante activities.

"Snap—"

"Nope." He shook his head. "No. Your involvement in that stopped in that warehouse. It's over for you now."

"But it's not over for you," I said quietly. "And we're right now finding our way to the us I think it's clear both of us want, so if you're gonna be a part of my life, what's part of your life will be part of mine."

"Is it clear?" he asked.

"Sorry?" I asked back.

"The thing that you said I really wanna get into, Rosie, is that you'd started falling for me. Considering what put us here, I felt it was priority to state you got nothing to worry about with Valenzuela and Bounty. But now we're there."

"I'd rather clear things up about Valenzuela and Bounty," I replied.

"Baby, are you falling for me?"

It was a whisper, soft and sweet with snowy, blue eyes intent on me, like the next words I spoke were the words he'd been waiting for since he'd started breathing.

"You're...you're..." God! "You're Snap."

His tone was the same when he confirmed, "I am but that doesn't answer the question, Rosie."

My tone matched his when I returned, "To me it does."

His snowy blue eyes started flaming as he muttered, "Fuck, now I'm not hungry and instead I wanna jump you through the butter chicken."

From what I'd eaten, I could tell the food he got was crazy-good and I'd been hungry.

But now I wasn't. I also wasn't feeling nervous or shy. I just wanted him to jump me.

Even so, we needed to stay on target.

"I don't want you to think I'll find someone else when I'm with you," I whispered.

"Rosie, do you think I'd be sittin' right here...hell, *you'd* be sittin' right here if I thought that?"

That made sense.

But still.

"I need you to know. I need to say the words. I need you to understand I know that was there and how it happened and it's still all about you. It was messy and crazy and scary but you came through all that, solid and strong and protective, and it became about that. But it feels wrong because it was all the first parts."

"It's not wrong, Rosalie."

"I want to make sure you believe that."

"I can assure you, baby, that I believe that."

I wished that worked.

It just didn't.

Not for me.

Because I knew how it was supposed to be.

"My mom…my dad…" I shook my head hard, trying to shake some sense into the words I had to say so he'd understand how important they were, "there was no one else for her and no one else for him. It wasn't about being a couple and forsaking all others. When they got together, the world just vanished. They functioned in it and I came along and they made me part of their world, but it was just us. There was family and there were friends, but in the end, it was just us. They never shared, either of them, but at least for Mom, outside going to the prom with somebody, I don't think there was anyone before him for her. I know my grandparents were freaked he was so much older than her but then Dad was Dad and he won them around."

"You cannot live your parents' life, honey," he said gently.

I nodded. "No, I get that. I totally do. That's not what I'm saying. I'm saying I'd want the man I decided on to know there was no one for me but him. That I want our lives and our children to be our world. I want the end result of what they had but it's not even that. I'd want my man to know down to his bones that was what he was getting from me."

"And you think, we go to that place, because of how this began, I'll question that," he deduced.

"I think you're brothers with Shy, so that history is just plain in your face, and then I was with Beck when things started, and I think life happens, arguments happen, and it would kill me if anything ever shook your understanding it's only you."

"Baby, when we make love later, you're gonna find out I'm not comin' to you a virgin."

I put my plate to my lap, leaned his way and said, "It's not *the same.*"

"I been along for this ride with you, Rosie. Do you think I missed that?"

"No, it's just—"

"I'm totally fuckin' in love with you."

I leaned back and stared, a flare happening around my heart that started to spread throughout my chest cavity.

"Gone, babe. *Gone,*" he continued. "You're sweet and you're funny and you're not selfish. How you could think that, I do not know, seein' as you put your ass on the line to save the soul of the man you were living with."

As much as I was rejoicing in what he'd said to me, I had to lay out where all that was at.

"That wasn't just for him, Snap, it was also for me."

"All right, if you told tell me there is some form of pure altruism out there, Rosalie, I'll tell you you're wrong because it doesn't exist. Even if you get nothin' outta something good you do, you still get the satisfaction that you're the kind of person who would do it. So in the end, that's getting something. So yeah, part of your angle was to get something outta that. You also got your face fucked up and your ribs busted. You knew that was a possibility and instead of getting shot of that guy, you carried on. So what do you think that says to me?"

"I was with that guy," I replied. "The wrong guy."

"No," he denied, beginning to sound impatient. "It says if you care about someone, it's not about going that extra mile. It's about giving everything. Honest to God, I fell in love with your tits and your hair and that beautiful voice and the way of you that I've learned recently you got from your mother and that cute-as-fuck skip-walk you got goin' on first, Rosie. But after that, all that is you filled in the rest and I don't give that first fuck he was there in between. He isn't anymore. And that's where we are now. He doesn't factor to me. He only factors to you and you've gotta let that go, Rosie. Because for me it's already gone."

"I get into this with you and later, it comes back to haunt me, that would not be good, honey," I pushed.

"It won't."

"You can't tell the future, Everett."

"When it comes to you, I can," he declared, all flinty. "We're gonna finish this conversation and the food. Then we're gonna go upstairs and finish what we started this morning. Tomorrow, we're gonna wake up and do more a' that. Repeat for eternity, tossin' in a couple of kids along the way. That's our future, Rosie. And just to make that clear, knowin' now you're falling for me, my world shrank to what's on this couch the minute with both sat on it but you should know, my world started shrinking long before that. And I'm not only good with that, it makes me really, fuckin' happy."

Right then, I was really fucking happy too.

"I have a feeling," I whispered, the words uneven from the emotion stuck in my throat, "that you're not gonna let me pay rent."

A smile bloomed on his face, huge, handsome, amazing.

He knew I was happy too, finally allowing myself to reach for it, and he was right about there not being any pure altruism because he also knew he gave me that, and he got something huge out of it.

That was what made him happy.

The chance at a shot of making me happy.

God, that was all just *so Snapper*.

"You wanna exercise your independence, we'll negotiate somethin' that makes you feel easy about that but you can still buy garden furniture. The bed, babe, that's not gonna happen since, if shit works out the way it should, I'll be in it as much as you, so that's on me."

"Are you saying that you wanna…" I swallowed, happy we were there, no…thrilled, but this was maybe too fast, "move in together?"

He shook his head. "Nope. I think you need some time and space, and we got more gettin'-to-know-you shit to do. But yeah, obviously eventually. Definitely."

And with that, Snap shoveled in more food.

I called his attention back to me. "Snap, Valenzuela and Bounty."

"Babe—"

"It worries me."

He gave me a thorough look and I could tell he was thinking deeply about this.

It took two mouthfuls of rice and korma with a chaser of a bite of tikka masala coated naan for him to come to a conclusion about what he was going to say.

"You know Chaos has been patrolling our turf now for well over a decade."

I didn't know that.

"Okay," I replied.

"Nothing has happened, Rosie. Not even close. Before Valenzuela, patrol wasn't even that big of a deal because everyone doin' stupid shit in Denver knew to keep it off Chaos. We just did it regularly to make sure that message stayed out there."

"Okay," I repeated.

He studied me again while he was eating and I took another bite too while he did it.

Finally, he pressed forward.

"Before my time, when they were pullin' outta some shit they were into, they lost a man."

Uh-oh.

"Good guy," he carried on, "way everyone tells it, the best."

"Snapper," I whispered.

"And I tell you that, Rosalie, because that loss did two things. It tore apart every member who stayed in the club and it solidified the brotherhood as well as the path they were on to get clean. I know that's a dichotomy but it's the way the story is told and it's the brotherhood I know. So what I'm sayin' is, that last part, we got in hand, but that first part, every brother is going to do everything in their power not to let that happen again."

"Not everything is in Chaos's power," I pointed out.

"That man they lost, name was Black, he had a woman and two boys."

Uh-oh!

"She's Chaos lore too, baby," he went on gently. "The way it's told, she never got over that and they loved their brother, they loved that woman, they loved those boys, so they felt his loss three ways. So when I say we're gonna do everything in our power not to lose anything precious along the way, we're gonna go balls to the wall with that."

He didn't lean into me but the way he was looking at me changed so it made it feel like he'd slid across the couch and got in my space.

"We are not doin' this stupid. We're playin' this smart. Those men have women and children to protect, Rosalie. I know you get that Club is a family, but maybe you don't get that Club is *family*. We want this done and we're all in to do it, but we're not gonna Butch and Sundance this shit. We all got different parents but we share blood. Chaos is our blood, baby, and I'm not sayin' shit isn't intense. I'm sayin' we're not taking unnecessary chances. And I can't tell the future. What I'm askin' is for you to trust me."

"I trust you, Snapper."

"Then all we got left is to eat and then we can go upstairs."

"There's nothing you have for the agenda?" I asked.

"Nope," he answered.

Well, that was a relief.

"We have something else to talk about," I shared as he shoved food in his mouth.

"What?" he asked after he'd swallowed.

"I want you to get that what I'm gonna say is real and not about all you're giving me."

"What?" he repeated.

"And I'm worried it's too soon and you won't believe in it."

"Baby…" He was losing patience. "*What?*"

"I'm not falling for you," I told him.

A look came over his face that made me scramble to keep talking.

"I've already fallen in love with you."

He froze.

Solid.

Staring at me.

I sat.

Solid.

Staring at him.

Snapper broke the silence.

"Shit, fuck, we're gonna have to nuke it," he growled, practically threw his plate on the coffee table, yanked mine out of my hand and did the same, then pulled me out of the couch.

Before I knew what was happening, he was pulling me up the stairs.

"Snap!" I snapped.

He turned and I nearly collided with him but stopped because his hands came up, framed my face, and he bent low from his step above me to put his face in mine.

"You just gave yourself to me, Rosie, so I'm havin' you now and I don't give a shit the naan is never as good after it's microwaved."

I was wrong.

The fireplace was okay for setting a romantic mood.

But the best romance in the world was standing with your man's hands on you in the curve of a spiral staircase talking about microwaving naan bread.

I wanted to laugh. I wanted to throw my arms around him. I wanted to go up on my toes and press my lips hard to his.

I'd found the man who was perfect for me and he was *mine*.

I didn't get a shot to do any of that.

He dropped his head farther and kissed me.

It didn't even start sweet.

It started wet and hot and stayed that way until Snapper broke the kiss, let go of my face, but again grabbed my hand and pulled me up the rest of the stairs.

When we got up there, I was ready to yank off all my clothes, all his clothes, and go at it fast and furious.

But Snapper had other ideas.

Sure, he walked direct to the bed.

And sure, he got right on it.

That was, sitting on it and pulling me in his lap with both my legs to the side (not even any straddle action!).

He reached out, turned on the light, and came back to me.

"Snapper," I whispered, curling the fingers of one hand around the side of his neck.

"Rosalie," he whispered back, sliding his hand up my spine.

When his fingers made it into my hair and he didn't pull me down to his lips, I shared, "Mom and I bought condoms at Walgreens."

His eyes flashed. "Love a girl who's prepared."

"I'm not usually prepared."

"Strike that. Love my Rosalie was in the headspace to know this was gonna happen and she prepared for me. But just to say, baby, you never need to worry. I'll have that covered for us."

I had no doubt.

I stroked his whiskered jaw with my thumb and asked, "Are you gonna kiss me?"

"In a sec," he answered, his fingers in my hair, the tips of them stroking the edge of my hairline behind my ear.

It felt crazy-nice.

His tongue in my mouth on the stairs had felt better.

He did this for a while, staring up into my eyes, and I shifted in his lap.

"Honey—" I began to prompt.

"This is gonna be our first time, Rosie, so we're gonna remember it, and I want it to be worth remembering."

Oh God.

How much more perfect could he be?

"'Kay," I muttered. "Take your time."

He grinned.

And it got that much more perfect.

"Love you," he whispered.

And much, *much* more perfect.

"Love you too," I whispered back.

His hand fisted in my hair. "Yeah. And thank you for loving me."

Oh *God*.

And now he was even more perfect.

"I think that's my line," I retorted.

"Waited for you awhile, Rosie. So you'd be wrong."

I couldn't take anymore.

I dipped closer, sliding my hand up to cup his jaw.

"If you don't kiss me soon, I'm gonna go crazy," I told him in all honesty.

"Your ribs—" he began.

I cut him off. "I'll deal."

His expression started changing. "No you won't."

"Baby," I hissed, putting my lips almost on top of his, "shut up and *kiss me*."

He shut up.

And then he whipped me to my back on the bed, curling over me, and he *kissed me*.

He did not tear my clothes off.

I did not tear his off.

We kissed and we touched and we stroked over clothes, then under them.

After a while we kissed harder and deeper and we touched more and I pulled off his thermal. He drew away to yank off his boots and socks.

He came back and we kissed hotter and wilder and we touched hungrier. But I got the better end of that deal because his smooth, sleek, warm skin was under my hands, I could feel the power of the muscle underneath that heated silk, and with all the kissing and touching and *that*, suddenly I was all about making this something to remember and going at it hot and heavy.

And *fast*.

So I pushed up with my hips to roll him to his back, straddled him, sat up, and pulled off my thermal and cami.

Astride him in nothing up top but my bra, Snapper just wrapped his fingers around the skin at my waist and slowly slid them up.

I felt him straining against his fly between my legs but he took his time.

"Baby," I whispered.

He sat up, touched his mouth to mine, wrapped an arm around me then glided his free hand up to my breast.

He held the weight in his palm over my bra but did nothing else.

"Snapper, honey," I breathed, pressing and swirling my hips into his hardness.

"Rosie," he whispered back, his sweet baritone drifting all over me.

He used his arm at my waist to pull me back and dropped his head to my chest.

Unhurried, he slid it to the breast he was not holding, over the swell, then back again, this time tracing the edge of the lace with his tongue.

Now we were getting somewhere.

But he was still going slow.

Restlessly, I churned against his hips, stroking his hair, his back, arching into his touch.

"I'm not real sure I can do slow," I told him breathlessly on the backward glide of his tongue.

"No?" he asked my skin.

"No," I murmured.

"Hmm…" he hummed against my skin.

God!

He was driving me crazy!

I ground into him, bunching his hair in my fingers, my mouth opening to say something (maybe whine, maybe beg, I was up for anything that might work at that point) when suddenly he tore the cup of the bra down and honed in with thumb and forefinger, twisting gently, just as he sucked my other nipple into his mouth over the bra.

The awesomeness of that tore through me. I jerked in his hold and he held me to him before he switched nipples and hands and then he was mouth-to-mouth on me.

Way.

More.

Awesome.

"Snapper," I moaned.

He sucked. He swirled. He rubbed me with the front of his teeth. And I rolled in his lap, pressing into his cock, doing all I could to stroke it with the crotch of my jeans.

He let my nipple go, pulled my mouth down to his, and kissed me hot and wet before he broke it and ordered gruffly, "Baby, get on your feet."

I didn't want to get on my feet.

I wanted to get him *in me*.

But I got on my feet.

I'd barely got my trembling legs to support me before his hands went to my fly.

Okay, this was good. I was happy to be on my feet for this.

The zip went down then my jeans went down.

My panties, thankfully, went down with them.

I stepped out of them hurriedly.

Snap surged up out of the bed.

"No!" I cried, landing both hands on his broad, bared shoulders and pressing down. "We're both getting farther away from where we're supposed to be."

He gave me a look that would melt asphalt at the same time it was filled with humor that I decided in an instant I utterly *adored* before his fingers went to the button on his jeans.

He grabbed his wallet before he shoved them down.

He stepped out of them, opened his wallet, pulled out a condom, and tossed his wallet to the nightstand.

"Hurry," I urged, not caring that I did it staring greedily at the perfection of the cock that had sprung free from his jeans and was now standing full and hard and proud, reaching toward me.

"Babe, hurrying a condom is a bad thing," he muttered, sounding growly turned on and amused, and I utterly adored that too.

I reached out and spread my hands across his pecs, touching him and watching him roll the condom on his beautiful, thick cock, all the way down to the root, dancing lightly on my feet with anticipation, salivating, running my thumbs hard over his nipples.

Snap latched onto my hips and sank back down on the bed, pulling me into his lap, this time not with my legs to one side, but a knee to either side.

Now we were talking.

"I'll give you a foreplay blowjob our second go," I offered, aiming myself at that goodness.

"Foreplay for me with you essentially involves you lookin' at me, so that's unnecessary, but I'm not gonna say no," he replied, guiding me to his goodness but doing it way too damned slow.

"Snapper, hurry," I rushed.

Laugher in his tone now. "Rosie, it isn't going anywhere."

I grasped either side of his head and looked into his eyes.

"I want you," I whispered.

With a rumble I felt from scalp to toes, he pulled me down and filled me.

Snapper was finally inside me.

My head fell back, my hands slid down to clench his neck, and I started moving.

"Fuck...*me*," he groaned.

He didn't mean it that way, but all I could think was, *gladly.*

"Oh my God, you feel..." I started on an upward glide, "*beautiful*," I ended on a puff of breath on a downward one.

He held me steady, arched away from him, riding his cock, with an arm slanted along my back and alternately played with my nipples and sucked them while I rode.

Which made me ride faster.

"Careful, honey," he murmured.

He was worried about my ribs, but...

No fucking way.

We were making this one to remember and we were going to do it in a way we'd never, ever forget.

I went faster.

"Jesus, Rosie," he grunted.

"God," I pushed out, loving the heft of him inside me, the support of his arm around me, the smell of him all around me, feeling it build in me.

I went faster.

"Jesus, fuck, *Rosie.*"

From every word he said it dripped that I was building it in him too.

And I *loved that.*

I snapped forward, my hair going everywhere, all around me, all around his face and shoulders, and I took his mouth in a hard kiss.

Then I gasped down his throat as he clamped an arm around my hips. Keeping me full of him, he shot up to his feet then turned and we were down and he was the one taking the ride.

I wouldn't have believed it, but this was even better.

I wound my legs around him, one at his waist, one at his thigh, and lifted my hips to take him as deep as he could go.

His hand went between us, his finger hit the spot, and I moved my hands to his hair, clutched both into the length and whimpered, "*Snap.*"

"Rosie," came his guttural reply.

And with that I was gone, flying, soaring, reaching for the stars, feeling Snap take his weight fully into his forearms on either side of me so all I took of him was him bucking between my legs. I heard his sharp grunts followed by a long groan and I felt him touching the heavens right there with me.

He stayed deep and I'd wrapped everything I had around him, holding him to me, when I came down, feeling his breaths hot and hard against the skin of my neck.

"That was awesome," I breathed.

"Yeah," he agreed.

"Totally awesome," I decreed.

On a small lurch of his body that told me he thought I was funny, he repeated in a voice that shared the same thing, "Yeah."

"Snapper?" I called.

He lifted his head, adjusted an arm so he could stroke my neck with his thumb, and looked me in the eyes.

"Yeah, baby?"

"It worked out in the end," I told him.

"What?" he asked.

"I found the one who was perfect for me."

He didn't seem sated or amused or anything right then.

He stared down at me under him, his body connected with mine, and he looked at me in a way that I knew that earlier, he had not lied.

I was his world.

So yeah.

Definitely.

Perfect for me.

Then he spoke, and as was Everett "Snapper" Kavanaugh's wont, he made it even better.

"I know the feeling."

Chapter Eight

Eden

Rosalie

"Rosalie."

I knew what that meant, Snap saying my name in that low, throaty tone. We'd had weeks now of me learning what that meant.

And even though I liked what I was doing, since he was Snapper and I'd give him anything, I slid his rigid, pulsing cock out of my mouth, slithered up his body, attached my lips to his, accepted his tongue as it slid between, thrilled in the bristles of his whiskers scratching my skin, and allowed him to roll me onto my back.

After a time, he broke the kiss and reached for a condom.

I explored the muscled contours of his back with my fingers, reveling in the power of his body under my touch and intensity in his profile that met my eyes while I did.

His eyes came to mine as his hand went between our legs and he just gazed at me, showing me openly so many things, all with just a look, it was insanity.

He was excited. He loved having me under him. He enjoyed what I'd done to his cock. He couldn't wait to get inside me.

And he loved me.

"Love you," I whispered.

"Love you too, Rosie," he whispered back right before he slid inside me.

At the glory of taking him, having him become a part of me, I closed my eyes.

Snap stroked his hands down the backs of my thighs, pulling them up as he went, until he reached my knees. He positioned them high at his sides, all this while he moved inside me.

Snapper Kavanaugh was a gentle lover. He liked slow. He liked taking his time. He liked building things until they were burning bright. He liked to be in the moment, not lost to it. And he guided me there right with him.

So he moved inside me, deliberate, leisurely, making sure I felt it as I took every inch of his length again, then again, and again, all the while watching me.

Finally, he started kissing me and then he worked my neck and he continued to hold the backs of my knees to control me, hold me back from careening into a place he didn't want us to be, and he made me just feel it. Feel us. His weight. Our bodies' movements. Our connection surging and retreating. Surging and retreating. *Surging.*

Through this he tuned to me, built it in me, in both of us, but he knew when he got me there. The kisses became less gentle penetrating strokes of the tongue, light tastes in the mouth. They drew deeper, twining and joining. But it was never ravishing. Snap didn't tongue fuck my mouth. Snap didn't fuck at all. With Snap, it was about being fully aware of the togetherness we were sharing and savoring it in every detail.

It was when the kisses heated up that the strokes of his cock got faster, the intensity built. Then he released my knees and let me go to devour him, biting and sucking his neck, his lower lip, sinking my nails into his flesh, digging my heels into his ass to get more of him, and more, and more, more, *more* until I flew high, anchored by his body, his love, his safety.

Which was what happened, or a version of it, no matter if he was on top, I was on top, I was on my knees, I was against the wall or bent over the back of the couch or whenever and wherever we did it (and once the gates were opened, we did it a lot).

Totally, if Snap was a different kind of guy, the Sting version of a biker, he'd go tantric. For real.

But he wouldn't make me do that.

And by the time we got there, no…by the time he took me there, he was so wound up by what I gave him, but I sensed it was more what he'd given me, that his explosion was—there was no other way to describe it—*immaculate.*

Muted in noise, concentrated in feeling, his fierce hold on me, the way he stilled buried deep inside me, it was like he reached out and drew the edges of the very air around us close, forming a little shell where it was only him and me and making love and finally climaxing.

Shy was an amazing lover.

Beck was no slouch either.

But I'd never had this. I didn't even know this existed.

What I knew now was that I couldn't live without it. Not just the "it" of it, sharing that "it" with Snapper.

"You good?" he whispered, nuzzling my neck.

Was I good?

The way it was at all times with Snapper, I knew now I'd never be bad.

No matter what life threw at us we'd always make it.

Because he'd make it so we would.

"I'm good," I whispered back, nuzzling his neck too and holding him to me in all the ways I could, even after he naturally withdrew from inside me.

If he finished on top, he always gave as much of his weight to me as he sensed I could bear, and fortunately with my ribs close to fully healed, I got to take more and more of him.

But once he did that, he didn't leave me.

This was something else Snap did. I didn't know if he preferred the sex or the intimacy of snuggle time after (okay, he was a guy so it was the sex, but the other was a close second).

He didn't rush either.

We didn't talk much. But we touched. We kissed. We held. We nestled and cuddled and caressed and squeezed.

But even if we didn't talk much after sex, make no mistake, Snapper Kavanaugh was a talker, and he spoke in two languages, the one where he just used his mouth and the one where he used absolutely everything.

But even good things had to end, so that morning, like every morning we'd had when we took what was between us where it was meant to be, had to end.

"I gotta get going," he muttered.

"'Kay," I muttered back.

He pulled his face out of my neck. "You're dinner shift tonight, yeah?"

I nodded. "Be home around eleven."

"You still on to go look at that property with me tomorrow?"

I grinned up at him, excited to be in on the ground floor of one of his investments. "Definitely."

"Good," he replied, dipped in, gave me a gentle but thorough kiss, then he rolled off of me.

I shifted to my side and watched him walk naked to the bathroom.

He had his Chaos emblem tat on his back and the Chaos scales with its reaper drifting up from one plate of the scales, the blood dripping from the other that I knew all the men had wherever they wanted to put them, his was along his ribs on his right side.

And down his left side, ribs to waist, in a simple, small, no-nonsense font, he had Henley's *Invictus* inscribed.

Out of the night that covers me,
Black as the Pit from pole to pole,
I thank whatever gods may be
For my unconquerable soul.

In the fell clutch of circumstance
I have not winced nor cried aloud.
Under the bludgeonings of chance
My head is bloody, but unbowed.

Beyond this place of wrath and tears
Looms but the Horror of the shade,
And yet the menace of the years
Finds, and shall find me, unafraid.

It matters not how strait the gate,
How charged with punishments the scroll,
I am the master of my fate:
I am the captain of my soul.

I hadn't known what it was (Snap had to tell me).

Even so, the minute I'd read it, the morning after our first night together, I'd touched my lips to it.

I'd had no questions about it. It said it all and what it said defined Snapper.

I knew Snap had not lived in night with demons plaguing him. He had not suffered evils. He had not endured untold tortures. He had fought no bloody battles. And God willing, he never would.

He had a good family who loved him, found another one who did the same, then won the heart of a woman who, day by day, became more tied to him.

But he was so self-contained. So self-aware. So self-assured. I knew deep into my soul that he could be delivered direct to the gates of Hell, and with head high and shoulders straight, he'd walk right through without a blink of his eyes or even a moment's hesitation.

It was just the man he was.

That wasn't right.

It was just the man that *my man* was.

When he'd told me what that poem was, not wanting me to worry, he also told me it meant nothing in regards to his history. It was just the series of words that was the favorite he'd ever read. It spoke to him and he wanted it on him to remind him of the power of those words, and if the time should come for him, it would serve to remind him to be that man.

I did not tell him he already was that man. I hoped he'd never have to find out.

But if he came to a time where he'd be tested, I knew he would then know the man he was, the man he was to me.

In a miracle of goodness, as miracles tend to be, with all of Snapper's autonomy, I did not feel left out.

In the weeks since we'd officially begun, it was not unusual I came home from a shift to find Snap stretched out on my couch reading. He wasn't about meeting me at the door and dragging me up the stairs to have sex with me.

He was about me settling in with a beer or a cup of herbal tea, tucked into him in front of the fire, me quiet and unwinding, Snap into his book but still right there with me. And then when it was time, we'd shut down the house, together, and move up the stairs, together, and find our way to the bed...

Together.

He hadn't lied. I was his world.

It was just a quiet, unhurried world where a roof over our heads and closeness (and a cozy fire) were all that was needed.

I was quiet too. I always had been. I wasn't attracted to bikers because they were (stereotypically) tough and wild and partying, all about loud music, loud pipes, good times, and loose women. I also wasn't attracted to bikers (just) because of my dad.

It was the family of a club. The closeness of the brothers. But also, if you found the right one, and in the end, I had, it was about strength and protection and loyalty. The fiercest, truest loyalty I'd seen in my life had always been demonstrated by bikers.

I'd just found the exact right fit for me.

I snoozed while Snap showered but he woke me before he went, moving my hair off my neck and kissing me there.

I slid my eyes up to him.

"Have a great day, Rosie," he bid softly.

"You too, honey," I replied.

He touched his mouth to mine and moved away.

I rolled to my other side so I could watch him spiral down the stairs.

I had not been to wherever he lived (because he always came to me). We had not gone on an official date, but we'd spent every night together. We'd gone out to no dinners, but had shared all we could when I wasn't working. We'd gone to see no movies, but had watched several.

Snapper Kavanaugh and Rosalie Holloway were about a little carriage house tucked far back from a city street, in our little Eden, insulated and isolated from the outside.

Perfect for Snap.

And as with everything I had with Snap, perfect for me.

* * * *

I was getting ready for my shift, still bartending, but I'd be on the floor starting the next week.

I was looking forward to hitting the floor because I got paid more for bartending in the paycheck department, but I could earn a mean tip, and if I was ever going to give Snapper his reading nook and myself some garden furniture, I had to be making a lot more than I was right then making.

So I was stroking on mascara, oblivious to the fact all the discoloration and bruising was long gone. My nose was back to normal. There was a split in my eyebrow, that break and the line that created it was still pinkish, but it was lessening.

None of this factored for me.

I was just putting on mascara.

And that was when the phone rang.

The screen came up with a number not known to me and I didn't know what drove me to answer it. I never answered calls that I didn't know the caller because in most cases, they were marketing calls and no one liked the aggravation of marketing calls.

But I answered the phone.

And it would take a great deal of time for me to make the decision if I was glad I did, or wished I hadn't.

"Hello?" I greeted.

"Rose, it's me."

My head dropped and I looked at the basin.

Beck.

I said nothing.

"I don't got a lot of time. We don't get a lot of phone calls and there's a line behind me and they aren't real patient."

"Beck—"

"I seriously fucked up and I know it."

God.

He so did.

But it was also *so* over so it didn't matter.

"Beck—"

"Turned my stomach, layin' hands on you. Almost got sick, watchin' the boys go at you. Thought it was Cage you were doin' it for and that was the only reason I got that fire in my belly, thinkin' all we had was a lie and all the time we had together, your heart was with him. Still, shoulda never took it there. Never put my hands on a woman like that. Never thought I could be a man who would do that to a woman. Especially not the woman who meant somethin' to me. Lay in this joint every night, not sleepin', can't get that shit outta my head, what I did to you. What I let them do to you. Even during the day, if I don't fight it back, it gets stuck in my throat so bad, I can't breathe."

There was something there that he gave me, knowing this. Knowing I had not made an entirely stupid-ass decision letting him into my life and heart.

It still didn't matter.

"Okay, but Beck—"

"I love you."

Oh no.

"Beck," I whispered.

"And I'm sorry."

That had my head snapping up and I stared at the mirror unseeing, all his words during this phone conversation spiking through me.

"Beck—" I began urgently.

"Find a good one next time, baby," he whispered, and now his words sent a chill through me.

"Beck!" I cried.

But he was gone.

I fumbled the phone, managing somehow to call Snapper.

It rang only twice when he answered, "Yo, Scully."

"Beck just called," I rushed out.

"Say again?" he asked, not sounding happy.

"I think from jail," I told him.

"Jesus Christ," he bit.

"No, Snap, he's done something or he's going to be doing something."

"Honey, I told you that—" he began.

"No, no, no!" I cut him off frantically. "He said he loved me and he was sorry and he told me to find a good one and then he hung up on me."

Snapper was silent.

Totally.

Just what I thought.

Damn it!

"Snapper!" I cried.

"Let me make some calls," he said.

"He's gonna rat," I declared.

"Keep calm, Rosie, and let me make some calls."

"It's okay for me to do it, I mean, not okay as we learned all too well, but it is *not* okay for a brother to rat, Snapper."

"Rosie, honey, let me go so I can make some calls."

"He'll be dead in a week."

"Baby, letting you go now."

"Get word to him. Tell him not to do it. Tell him *I* told him not to do it."

"Okay."

"This isn't about him," I said hurriedly. "It is, but it isn't. In the world we live in, he can't right the wrong he did me unless he lets justice serve. But not this way, Snap. Not this way."

"I hear you, Rosie," he said gently. "Now I gotta let you go, baby."

"Okay, Snap."

"Call when I know something," he said.

"Okay."

"Love you," he finished.

"Love you too," I replied.

He disconnected and I found it difficult to focus on mascara.

"I am the master of my fate: I am the captain of my soul," I whispered to my reflection, trying to get a hold on the panic. It just didn't work when I concluded, "The problem is, so is he."

* * * *

I pretty much barreled down the drive at eleven-oh-seven that night, coming home after my shift, touching the garage door opener and making the swing into the garage.

And Snapper did not stay laid out on the couch with his book, only to look over the top of it when I hit the living room and give me warm, happy-you're-home, now-get-over-here-and-cuddle-with-me eyes.

I hadn't even pulled into the garage (next to his truck, by the way, he now had the second remote) when I saw him in the doorway to the kitchen.

"No, no, no, no, no," I chanted.

I couldn't have my phone on me at work but I'd checked it during a break and I had a message from Snap saying he was still looking into things. But when I'd gone to get my purse after shift was over, I had another message from Snap saying, "I got the details, baby. Don't think about it. It might not be as bad as you think. I'll share when you get home."

I did not drive home like the devil was on my heels because first, Snapper was there and it was worth getting home healthy and all in one piece, and second, I was not a big fan of drivers who drove like wherever they were going was more important than anything else happening on the planet, so I refused to be one of those kinds of people.

Nevertheless, I didn't dawdle.

After I parked, I grabbed my purse and hurried out of my car, not liking that Snapper was in the kitchen doorway waiting for me.

He'd said it might not be as bad as I think.

Him standing in the doorway made me think it was worse than I thought.

"Hey," I called, slamming my car door.

"Hey, darlin'," he called back.

I rounded the hood of my car. "Why are you waiting in the doorway?"

"Because I'm worried about your frame of mind," he told me.

"My frame of mind was controlled until I saw you standing in the doorway."

His lips quirked and that finally set my mind at ease.

He got out of the way in order for me to be able to get inside, but also for him to be able to walk to the fridge to grab me a beer. He didn't even offer tea.

He also didn't give me a welcome home kiss.

This was bigger than tea, which was bad.

But Snap meeting me at the door and not giving me a kiss?

Okay, now my mind was no longer at ease.

He uncapped a Fat Tire for him, a Blue Moon for me, handed me mine, and then he leaned a hip against the countertop.

I didn't take a pull of my brew.

I looked into his eyes.

"Talk to me," I demanded.

"Took me a while to get it because it isn't intel the cops want out there, but I got it. Throttle turned."

"He what?"

"Turned. Switched sides. He's now a CI."

Oh my God.

I watched TV. I knew what that meant.

"A confidential informant?" I asked to confirm.

"Yeah. Keepin' him on the inside, they're gonna find some loophole or technicality to let his ass go. He returns to what's left of Bounty. Bounty, from all reports, regardless that shit has already got their ass in a sling and their charter is in danger of getting yanked because of it, is returning to working whatever they're working, including Valenzuela. Since that's apparently gonna happen inevitably, while it happens, Throttle digs as deep as he can get and he gives them everything he's finding."

"Holy crap," I whispered.

Snapper nodded. "It's dangerous as fuck. And baby, warning, the degrees a snitch can be a snitch are many, none of them popular, and that's the highest degree you can get. If he's about atoning, that motherfucker is all in."

That was when I took a pull from my brew.

A long one.

"He also promised to keep Bounty off you."

I nearly choked on Blue Moon.

I swallowed with difficulty and Snap kept going.

"It's covered, as I explained, but he's added insurance. And, babe, before you let this sink in too deep and it messes with your head, there is no doubt from that phone call he's doin' this for you, but he's also getting immunity and if the shit he gets on Valenzuela is good enough, WITSEC."

"Witness protection?" I breathed.

Snap nodded. "Valenzuela is not only a big fish, he's linked to bigger fish. This operation could go on months, maybe longer, and crack a lot of shit wide open. Throttle offers up something juicy, he'll have to testify against them, and he'll get protection."

"How protective is witness protection?" I inquired and Snap grinned.

"I read a lot, Rosie, but not sure I've read any stats on how many bad guys turned snitch got hunted down for vengeance. Though, I know they don't offer that shit random and definitely not generously. If they give it, they intend for it to do what it's supposed to do. So he'll slide right off the grid in a way it'll take some doing for anyone to find him."

I drew in a big breath, then let it out.

"You need to know something."

The way Snapper said that didn't do anything to my finally calming frame of mind.

"What?" I asked.

"This was our plan all along."

I stared at him.

"Chaos wanted him to turn," he explained.

Oh God.

"You knew that?" I queried.

Slowly, he nodded.

"You told me that it was about shutting down the shipments," I reminded him. "Messing with Valenzuela's distribution. Showing Bounty the worst of it and pulling them back to the right side."

"Rosie, baby, if you'll remember, I did share that we wanted those boys in the joint so pressure could be put on them to do the right thing, and having one of Bounty turn and work with the cops would definitely be the right thing. That said, Tack always wanted more pressure put on Throttle because he figured the man would do what he could to keep you, absolutely keep close to you and not take semi-permanent residence in the clink. He just needed the right incentive to get his head out of his ass and do it. Obviously, all this was supposed to go down without Throttle knowing you helped put his ass in a cell. But that was our ultimate goal."

I turned my head to look out the window but didn't see anything, considering I was taking another deep pull of my beer and not liking the thoughts barreling in my brain.

"Rosie," he called, his tone searching and sweet.

I returned my attention to him.

"Why didn't you tell me?"

"Because that was Chaos's goal. My goal was for you to realize he was an asshole and dump him so I could have a clear go."

It took a second for his words to hit me.

And when they did I nearly busted out laughing.

I managed not to do that but I couldn't stop myself from smiling.

Snap smiled back, so Snapper, not hiding from me he was relieved.

Or how deeply.

But his smile didn't last long.

"Valenzuela has disappeared," he announced.

I'd been about to take another fortifying slug from my beer, but what he said made me stop.

"What?"

"No one has seen him in weeks. Weeks that are now becoming months."

"Whoa," I whispered.

"Yeah," he agreed.

"What does that mean?" I asked.

"We have no fuckin' clue," he answered.

"Are you thinking things are better or worse without him?"

"I'm thinking things are uncertain without him. They weren't entirely certain with him, the man is messed right the fuck up. There was always no telling what he would do, just that whatever he did would be what we know of him. Messed right the fuck up. But at least he was visible, around, and although his operation is tight and him being around didn't give us dick, something is better than nothing. Him disappearing off the planet is just nothing, and nothing in this situation is not good. Uncertain nothing is definitely not any better."

"That doesn't sound real great," I noted in an understatement.

"It isn't," Snap unnecessarily agreed. "But even so, him bein' gone does not mean his operations have ceased. His crew is still at it like he was in the driver's seat, full bore."

"Do you know what that means?" I asked.

He shrugged. "Either he's callin' the shots remotely, or he's put someone in charge. We don't got much of a handle on it, neither do the cops, and that's making everyone twitchy."

I was feeling twitchy right along with them and I didn't really understand what was happening.

It struck me belatedly he was sharing this with me.

And cautiously, I brought that to his attention. "I thought we weren't going to talk about this kind of thing."

"Well, I'm deep in this and your ex is now deeper in this. Not to mention, I had to come clean about what the Club was up to with your ex and I didn't know how you'd respond to that." He grinned. "So although I'm not gonna give you daily status reports, I never intended to keep you fully in the dark, so here's where we are now. Me, Chaos…and Throttle."

My Snapper was so awesome.

"Thank you, Snapper," I said softly.

"Don't mention it, Rosie," he replied.

"Though I think it's relatively weird I'm thanking you for not keeping me fully in the dark about a drug dealing, woman pimping, gun running, pornographic movie producing bad guy and my ex, who beat the snot out of me with his brothers, who now is putting his ass on the line for immunity and atonement, something *your* brothers essentially set him up to do."

His grin spread into a smile. "Yeah, baby. Now we know precisely how nice it is to have our little cloud of sweetness in the sea of all that crazy."

Oh man, did I know what he meant.

And I loved it that he felt like he was right there with me.

Cloud of sweetness.

That was almost better than Eden.

But Eden was paradise so I was going to stick with that.

"Yeah," I replied and then took a pull from my beer.

When I finished, Snap asked, "You good?"

I nodded.

He studied me. "You sure?"

I nodded again.

He inched nearer to me, reaching out a hand to tag the side belt loop on my jeans and pull me a lot closer to him.

Our bodies were inches away when he noted, "Rosie, you kind of freaked."

I was worried he'd worry about that. It wasn't done for a woman to get twisted up like that for an ex, and the road to our cloud of sweetness had been a pretty rough ride.

"Snap, I have no problem with him paying for what he did to me. But the punishment for that is not him getting shivved."

He started chuckling and through it muttered, "My Rosie sayin' 'shivved.' Too fucking cute."

I leaned into him, resting my weight on his body, smiling up at his handsome face. "I'm glad you think it's cute. But still, I don't want him shivved. And to come clean to you, he does good with this, my opinion is, he's atoned. And I hope that WITSEC is better than all those shows that have the mafia guys finding their prey and making them run for their lives."

There was a loaded moment of hesitation before Snapper replied, "Yeah, that guy was a massive dick and a serious moron, but can't help, he puts his ass out like this, to hope for that too." He ran an arm along my waist and pulled me closer, sadly saying, "Since we're into the heavy, might as well get it all out there."

Oh man.

"What?" I asked.

He didn't make me wait, and fortunately, it wasn't as heavy as he thought.

Then again, with the heavy we'd been talking about, it didn't get a lot heavier.

"Speck wants a word," he shared. "He was on you when you got taken and he feels shit how things went down with you. I've been holdin' him back because he was not my favorite person and I didn't want him anywhere near you. But things have settled, you're good, I need to let that go and he needs to say his piece so he can get that weight off."

"It wasn't his fault."

"He needs to say his piece."

"Okay, maybe we should have him over for dinner on one of my nights off."

"He doesn't need to say *that* much of a piece."

I started laughing.

Oh yeah.

Snap loved our little cloud as much as I did.

"Right, then we'll meet him for a drink or something."

"That'll work," he muttered.

"Is that it?" I asked.

"No," he answered.

Man!

I'd had a tough evening, on my feet making drinks, worried about Beck, now all was good (or good*ish*) I just wanted to finish my beer, make love to my guy, and go to sleep.

"What?" I prompted.

"Shy made an approach. He and Tab want things settled with all of us."

This confused me.

"Settled how?"

"Shy didn't do you right," he began to explain. "And by extension, Tab was involved in that. They feel that and have for a while, but definitely now that you're back in the fold. They want to make sure all is copasetic in the family."

"Well, I suppose we can all have a drink too, but that's still absurd."

"Sorry?" he asked.

"I dated Shy for what? A month or so? He broke it off with me, started it up with Tabby, they got married and had a baby. Sure, it hurt back then but back then was back then and I've moved on. It's not like Adam chucked Eve aside for a biker princess and they have to apologize to God. People get together. They break up. They move on. It is what it is and that was what it was and we're all someplace else now. No need to make a big thing about it."

"Fuck, how much more can I love you?"

I felt every one of those words sink right through my skin and make a beeline to my heart.

"That's so weird," I replied. "All the time I ask myself the same thing."

At my words, Snapper's entire demeanor changed and I had a feeling they'd found their way to his heart too.

And that made me happy.

"Time to finish your beer, Rosie," he declared.

I knew it wasn't time to finish my beer.

It was time to go up to bed.

Together.

So I did something I hadn't done since I was twenty years old.

I chugged an almost full beer.

Then I made out with my man in the kitchen with both of us smiling through it because Snapper clearly thought watching me chug a beer was funny and I was happy he thought I was funny.

I tossed my bottle.

Snap and I shut down the house.

And we headed up to bed.

Epilogue

"Master of my fate:
Captain of my soul"

Snapper

"Hey, honey."

Snap turned from marking the wall where he and Shy were going to mount the cupboard to see his Rosie strolling in with Kane, better known as Playboy since the kid, not but a few months old, was a damned flirt. The baby was on her hip.

He was Shy and Tab's little boy.

Tabby was following her toting a diaper bag, Tab's eyes going to her man, but Rosie's eyes were on Snap.

His woman looked seriously fucking good with a baby on her hip.

And she just looked seriously fucking good always.

Shy moved to Tab.

But Snap stood still because Rosalie was moving to him.

When she made it, he gave her a lip touch then gave Playboy a tickle to which the kid wobbled and gurgled but mostly just hung on to Rosie (this hanging on meaning grabbing onto her tit, freaking little flirt) and he looked back to his woman.

"What do you think?" he asked.

She took her eyes from him and looked to the cupboards Shy and him were installing.

It was his condo, where he lived. Or now, where he used to live.

Before Rosie, he'd spent most of his time in his room at the Chaos Compound, but if he felt the need to have quiet, get some space just to himself (which was not rare), he came there.

But since he now spent all his time with Rosie, he wasn't a big fan of having a property that he wasn't using that was also not doing anything for him. Seeing as he'd moved into the place as is and didn't do shit to update it when he did, but the building was a nice one and he could get decent rent if he fixed it up, he was putting in a new kitchen, new bathrooms, painting the walls, and tiling the floors.

And he'd been able to gut it and start doing that because the week before, he'd full-on moved in with Rosie.

Snap moving into their carriage house had been a hiccup in their lives, something that wasn't the same as every day before had been, but each day wasn't much different. Not to mention it hadn't taken much since most of his stuff he sold on Craig's List because with Rosie's stuff, and the extra she'd bought, the crib was sweet and they didn't need his shit messing with her mojo.

But all in all, that was the way they were. Each day bleeding into the next, nothing new (except a dining room table, garden furniture and his "reading nook"—something he thought was hilarious and cute—hilarious because the words were goofy as shit, cute because she thought of him, even if he still read most of the time camped on the couch because she could stretch out beside him).

But everything was solid. It was not good, but instead golden.

Rosalie Holloway was not about adventure and excitement. She was just about being with the people who meant something to her, dialing down the world so all you needed to feed your soul was an hour with her quiet, stretched out with you on the couch.

And learning that, Snapper had fallen in love with her even more.

"They look good," she declared, attention on the cupboards they'd already put in.

"You'd think that you picked them," Tabby replied to Rosalie and looked at Snap. "They are nice. I still think you should have gone with the cream."

"The place is modern, cream is more traditional," Rosalie said.

"Cream is more neutral," Tab returned.

Rosalie shot her a smile with her eyebrows raised. "More neutral than white?"

Snap was not a fan of the eyebrow raise only because it took his attention to the split in the left one.

Her scars were visible, thin white marks that ran through her brow, along her jaw, and one that was about a half an inch down the left side of the bridge of her nose.

Since they had the conversation now months ago, she hadn't mentioned them, and that was good.

But every time his attention was turned to them, he saw her on the floor of that warehouse, and that was bad.

He'd lied to her that night he came clean about what Chaos's real plans were with her ex. He did not think there was anything Gerard Beck could do to atone for what he'd done to Rosalie. He thought the guy was a useless piece of shit and apologies after you and your brothers delivered a beat down to a defenseless woman because you'd been caught breaking the fucking law were worthless—if they came in words, or if they came in deeds.

But Rosie seemed mellow about it, was definitely on the path of moving on from it and Throttle, and he wasn't about to do anything to bite into that.

"Need you to look at those tile samples, Rosie," he said to take his mind off that shit. "We need to make a decision so I can order it and get it delivered."

She nodded to him and moved with Playboy over to a box that had a cupboard in it that Shy and him hadn't taken out yet where there were a bunch of tile samples on top.

"The black," Tabby, having wandered over to have a look too, decreed.

"My woman's always got an opinion," Shy muttered through a smile, stripping the shrink wrap and protective covering off the cupboard they were about to mount.

"Gray," Rosalie said.

"Gray-shmay," Tabby returned. "Gray's boring."

"It's a rental, Tab," Rosalie replied in that sweet, lilting voice of hers, not upset in the slightest about Tab's outspoken ability to share her opinion. Then again, that was the way it was with those two, or Rosie with anybody. She didn't get wound up a lot. In fact, since she settled in after what happened to her, she never got wound up. "It needs to be neutral so people can build on it with their own things."

"You can build on black," Tabby said.

"And black shows everything. It's harder to keep looking nice," Rosalie retorted.

Tabby had nothing to say to that because Rosalie was right.

The gray it was then.

Needless to say, the women had become friends. Outspokenly opinionated or not, it was hard not to like Tabitha Cage. She was just good people. And if you were a woman, she was the best kind of friend you could have around (if often a nutcase, but since Rosalie was totally not, they evened each other out). And straight up with everything, it was impossible not to like Rosie.

They'd gotten close. It might have been about Rosie opening the doors for Tab to swoop in because she was worried after what had happened to Rosalie. Mostly it was about the fact that they all just liked each other. History didn't factor. It was just done in a way that there wasn't even awkwardness. There was just what they had now.

Furthermore, they were the generation of the brothers and their women in the Club that were around the same ages, so with Joke and Carrie, they hung together a lot.

Playboy reached out to his momma and Tabby took her son.

Rosie turned to Snap. "We came to check out the cupboards and look at the samples. We also came to see if you guys wanted to take a break and go out to lunch with us."

"Lunch sounds good," Shy replied, moving to his wife and son, and when he did, his boy lost interest in Momma and reached out to Daddy.

Shy didn't make him want. He took his little man and pulled him close, brushing his lips across the top of his cranium, then breathing in deep, like the essence of his son was the elixir of life.

And it probably was, something Snap looked forward to getting his own whiff of when the time was right.

"Joker, Carissa, and Travis are meeting us at Las Delicias in half an hour," Tabby told the men.

"Perfect," Snapper said, looking to Rosie. "You on the back of my bike, baby?"

She looked him right in the eyes.

"Absolutely."

At her word, the way it settled down low in his gut, he smiled.

He was that guy who'd always known his destiny. Whatever life smacked him with, he knew he'd deal with it while he headed unerring for one thing: keeping himself breathing while finding a woman to love and building a family.

He didn't give that first fuck if he did this rich or poor. He didn't care if he did it in Denver, where he'd grown up, or in Alaska, or on the moon. He'd liked school but when it was done, he was done with it. He didn't want to play a corporate game. He didn't want to face a life of monotony. And he made it so he had none of that. He just wanted family, his bike, his brothers, solid and steady.

But most important, he wanted a world where his woman looked him in the eyes when he asked her to be close to him, close to the man who wanted what many would consider as limits that were all of that, not riches in the bank, not vacations in Tuscany, just whatever life led them to, and her answer was, *Absolutely*.

He'd found it in Rosalie.

He had it in his home, in his bed, on the back of his bike.

It was a miracle, quiet and true and constant.

And no matter what he had to do to keep it…

He was not ever going to let it go.

* * * *

"Snap?"

"Yup?"

She was lying on him.

It was after lunch at Las Delicias with their crew. After he and Shy went back to the condo to finish with the cupboards and the women went where women went to work off burritos (in Rosie and Tabby's case, the mall). After he'd come home and showered and ate dinner with Rosalie then took her out for a ride in the early summer waning sun. After they'd returned home, got beers and stretched out on the couch, him with his book, her with hers that he'd noticed she was not reading, but he didn't think much of it. When she had a book of her own, her mind wandered often, but he could tell by the look on her face when it did, her reflections never took her anywhere she didn't want to be.

"You never said what you thought of the name Hermione."

He felt his body tense.

This happened right before it shook uncontrollably because he burst out laughing.

When he got some control over it, if not a lot, he saw her smiling down at him.

It was then he realized a promise he made her he was not keeping.

He'd told her that he was going to get her to a time in her life when she'd spend a lot of it laughing.

So far this hadn't happened.

Instead, she'd gotten him to a time in his life where he did that, no…she gave him that, and when she did, she just watched him, happy and smiling.

He again vowed to himself to do what he could to give that back.

But he had a feeling they both were totally down with the way it turned out.

When he finally got control of his humor, he lifted his brows and asked softly, his arm around her going tight, "You thinkin' about babies, baby?"

"Would that freak you?" she asked back.

"Fuck no," he answered firmly.

And earned another smile.

"Two for you too, or…?" she prompted.

"As many as you want, I'll give you," he replied.

The smile he got from that was seriously sweet in ways he felt the urge to do something about it.

"Rosie, Cotton's up to some serious shit. You need to let me finish this," he declared. "Then I'll spend time finishing you."

She turned her gaze to his book. "I'm always losing you to Steve Berry."

"The man puts one book out a year," he informed her.

She looked back to him but dipped her head sideways to his book. "How many times have you read that one?"

"Three."

And it finally came.

Her body moving on him with her laughter.

Still doing it, she propped her book up on his chest and ordered, "Finish your chapter." Her attention turned to her own pages. "Then you can finish me."

Snap also returned his attention to his book.

And he never read so fast in his life.

* * * *

Snapper was behind the bar at the Chaos Compound.

They had three new recruits who he could press into service, as was their duty, but he was playing bartender like he often played bartender—definitely since the shit with Valenzuela started—doing it keeping an eye on his brothers.

And now Rosalie.

She was on the couch in the corner with Speck, a Corona in her hand, a smile on her face.

Her mass of thick dark hair, her slim figure, her long legs, her pretty face, those warm hazel eyes, that fucking smile...

Yeah, he'd caught hold of a miracle.

Whatever they were talking about made Speck feel good and loose, in their own little world the only way Rosalie could give a man, though with obvious differences for Speck.

She had this knack, brother, old lady or biker groupie. Rosie was not one to slam tequila shots, get loud, move straight to crazy, then come on strong so he had no choice but to mostly fuck her against a wall on a trajectory to his room.

Quiet communion was where Rosie was at.

And if she wanted his dick, all she had to do was give him that look. The one she had that had two versions. And depending on the version, Snap could gauge where it was as to where they would go with it. If it was urgent, he'd get her ass to his room in the back of the Compound so he didn't make her wait to give her what she wanted. If it wasn't, he'd get her ass home.

He tore his eyes from Rosie and scanned the bar.

Boz was sitting a stool, pounding tequila shooters. Rough count, so far he'd had seven.

He was doing this staring at the bar and not being social in a way that wafted off him like a nasty cloud, warning everyone to stay away.

Not a single brother or any of their women were stupid, so they stayed away.

There were a lot of reasons for Boz's current disposition. But in his present mood, Snapper could not make an approach to try to pry out of him which one was fucking with his head right then and driving him to get shitfaced. Or worst case, if all of them were.

If the man wanted alone time, even if he was seeking that in a room full of people, Snap was going to give it to him.

So he let that go.

Big Petey was in a huddle at the far end of the bar with Dog and Brick.

Both Dog and Brick had left some time ago for the Western Slope to open up a new shop there. But now, both were back in Denver to help them concentrate on their troubles.

Brick would be taking off soon, though. He needed to get back. He'd found a woman worthy of him, a feat for Brick since most the women he chose fleeced his ass or ended up making a play at leading him around by his dick. All reports, this one was neither. This one was all good. She lived in a biker town called Carnal. The wedding was imminent, and for it, the brothers would soon ride.

Snap did not like the look of this huddle. Shit was serious and it wasn't getting any better mostly because it wasn't getting *anything*. Since Rosalie had taken her beating from Bounty months ago and Chaos rained down retribution, the only thing that had happened had been the fact that not too long ago, they got a delivery on their picnic table outside that very building.

But that had been some nasty shit and as such had sent all the brothers, already on edge, straight to the verge. Worse, they didn't even have enough a hold on what was happening to give it a damn good yank in an attempt to shake something loose.

No one wanted Armageddon.

But it was worse knowing it might be out there, waiting, and they had no choice but to wait for it to hit, a sneak attack.

That huddle could indicate sides were being taken even if the thing they most didn't need in the Club right then were lines being drawn. Snap felt a line had been drawn when Rosie had been pulled in then torn apart, it was just that after that had happened, in Snapper's estimation all the men had stepped to the right side of that line.

In its history, Chaos had splintered once. It got ugly. Right now, it could not splinter again. And even though every brother knew that to be true, with the shit going down, it seemed an inevitability.

On the fucking verge.

Tab and Shy were not there. Nor was Rush, Tabby's brother by blood, Snapper's brother of the cut. Tack and Tyra either.

Tab had recently sustained a loss. The night of the picnic table. She hadn't been back to the Compound since and was finding recovery difficult. So Shy, Rush, Tack, Tyra, and Tab and Rush's little half-brothers, Rider and Cutter, were seeing to their girl.

Another shot across the bow.

Yeah, on the goddamned verge.

Roscoe and Hopper were playing pool with Lanie and Carissa. Joke was in the garage across the forecourt, keeping his shit tight by letting his head fall deep in a build.

Lanie and Carissa were losing in a big way. Lanie and Carissa also did not care, their frequent laughter and bright personalities, along with Rosie's quiet serenity, were the only things that was keeping the doom hanging over the Chaos Compound from enveloping them, choking out the air, strangling them standing.

Snap saw it in Roscoe and Hop. The brothers shot smiles at the women but their bodies were tight. Of late, Roscoe had taken to habitually cracking his knuckles, and right then was no different. Hop had wound his head around to loosen the neck muscles twice that Snap had caught.

On the verge.

Big Petey moved from the huddle toward Renae, who was shooting the shit with Arlo on stools at the other end of the bar, close to the double doors that led to the Compound. This happened as Dog headed to the back hall, where he'd left his old lady, Sheila, in his room. His woman was undoubtedly passed out or simply physically immobile after the hard-core sex sounds they'd all heard drifting into the common room, prompting Snap to turn up the music. Brick's route was to the pool table.

Snap watched Pete's movements closely.

Arlo had a woman who he'd claimed as his for a long time, and Snap didn't know a lot about that, he just knew he stepped out on her. Frequently. After Boz (who also liked variable pussy even when his cock was owned by just one) left Bev, Arlo was the last brother with a Chaos patch who did that shit. And Snap had not left attention to Renae to that brother alone. He'd kept an eye.

He didn't like it.

Pete, it was coming clear, liked it less.

Then again, the look on Pete's face, the reason why Snap wasn't a big fan of Arlo setting up to make a move on Rosalie's mother was not why Pete didn't like it. Pete had around ten years on Arlo, but he wore it on his face more like it was fifteen. Or thirty.

But the man was the most loyal, solid human being Snap had ever met. More than Tack, who could be volatile, even if he had a fierce check on that shit. Even more than High, who'd learned the hard way to keep his shit cool. More even than Brick, who was mellow and smooth almost all the time, even if he hadn't just finished a blunt.

As Pete instigated a cockblock, Snap again scanned the space.

High and Millie had High's daughters that he'd had with his ex, so they were up in that crazy-ass mansion the man had bought his girls in north Denver.

Yeah, Logan "High" Judd was a biker who lived in a gothic Victorian manor that dripped class from every square centimeter, the same as his old lady. All of it, except the basement man-cave that was such a stark contrast to all that was around it, Snap couldn't walk into the fucking place without feeling an instant sense of culture shock, then fast on the heels of that busting a gut laughing.

Whatever they were doing up there, Snap had no doubt High often found times to reflect on current times, and when he did, he'd wind his neck around just like Hop.

Notably absent was Hound. He used to be around a lot. Serious shit had gone down with him—him and his brothers, him and his now-woman. Snap was frankly shocked as shit Hound had nailed down any woman at all, much less the one he went balls to the wall for. Snap was under the impression that the man had always been about brotherhood, blood, guts and attachment-less booty.

Then again, a lot had surfaced about Hound recently that was shocking as shit.

So in a rare instance, when it came to Hound, Snap had learned he was wrong.

But in this instance, he was glad to be that.

His eyes lit on Rosalie, and not unusually, his dick had the response.

She was mellowed out, with her people, but the vibe had penetrated, she knew what it did to her man, and she was all in to do something about that.

He lifted his chin to accept her offer.

She smiled and looked to Speck.

Snap moved to Boz and poured another shot in the empty shot glass Boz was scowling at.

Then he shouted, "Chill!" and the recruit that had been doing whatever the fuck he'd been doing behind the bar with Snap loped over.

"You got the bar," he said to the prospect.

"You got it, brother," Chill replied.

Snap moved around the bar and it was not a surprise to him that, in sync, he met Rosalie at the door that was the mouth to the back hall, the hall that led to all the brothers' rooms.

Returning her small grin, probably also returning the heat he felt from her eyes, he slid an arm around her shoulders and felt hers glide along his waist.

They had to turn slightly sideways to get through the door, but they did it, moving attached through it, down the hall and all the way to his room.

* * * *

He took her with two fingers, sucking rhythmically on her clit, but harder, then harder, and then harder, eyes up watching her strain into him, naked, arched, legs dropped wide to the sides.

As he intended, she found it for him, her body bolting against his mouth, and he kept sucking and stroking her through it until he knew it was too much and only then did he unlatch and lift away, still watching her, eyes glued to the beauty of his Rosalie gripped with an orgasm.

But he kept his fingers buried deep, part of her, and only when her frame settled and her gaze drifted hazily down her body to catch his did he come up on his knees, withdrawing his fingers slow, tender, floating them over her clit with a light touch, listening to the soft noise she made telling him she liked that.

He kept his eyes on his woman, her eyes on him, as he knelt between her legs, wrapping his left hand around his cock and stroking slowly while he lifted his right hand, fingers coated with her, and drew them into his mouth to suck her sweetness down his throat.

Another noise, a deeper mew, and she writhed in front of him.

He'd taken her there.

But she was ready for more.

He slid his fingers out between his lips and ordered gently, "Turn over, baby. On your knees."

She nodded and did as told instantly, offering her sweet ass and wet, pink cunt to her man, spreading her thighs to give him the perfect angle to position.

God, fuck, he loved this woman, her hair on his pillow, the smell of her sex in his nose, the quiet unity they shared all the time, but especially in these times, the straight-up trust she gave him all the time.

But especially in these times.

He wiped the wet of her from the whiskers around his mouth with the back of his forearm, not licking it clean but leaving it there so he could smell her on him after they'd passed out to sleep.

Then he walked on his knees to her, guiding his cock, now unsheathed since they'd both been tested and she started taking care of family planning.

He'd lay seed in her womb. Soon. After Chaos shit was finished and he could hand her nothing but steady and true.

The ring he'd give her, though, that'd come sooner.

He slid in slowly, watching her strain to hold back and take him how he wanted to take her. He knew his baby was wild in just one way and he gave her that, after he took her to a place where the end result would blow her mind but reduce their world to nothing, not a thing, but their two bodies in a bed.

He rocked in her, watching her arms come out, dig under the pillows, reach to wrap her fingers around the headboard.

And he continued to rock in her, giving her just his cock, not even caressing the skin of her beautiful ass with his fingers.

As he watched the tension gather in the muscles along her spine, felt her thighs and ass quivering as she took his slow thrusts, holding back for him, he went faster, catching her at the waist, pulling her to meet him.

"Snap," she whispered.

He said nothing. He was right there. Right where he was made to be. And she couldn't miss it.

But he bent over her, gliding his hands up her ribs and in. The light twists he gave her tight nipples caused her entire body to buck.

Christ, she was fucking magnificent.

"*Snap.*" It was a plea.

He dragged the pads of his thumbs hard over her nipples, then tweaked them with his thumbnails.

"Oh God, *baby*," she breathed.

Moving his hands, he held her with his left at her waist and flattened his right on the small of her back.

It was time.

"Go, baby," he whispered.

And she went. Head flying back, fingers tight around the headboard to give her leverage, Snapper watched her at first, fucking herself on his dick.

Then he watched their glistening connection as she drove back into him, again, again, again.

One of her hands released the headboard, dove between her legs, and Snap clenched his ass, then his entire body to beat back the rush of feeling that would overwhelm him if he let it as she rode his cock on her knees, touching herself. She didn't do this long before she cried out and kept at her rough ride through coming, coating him so fucking slick, they both had to be dripping.

Only then did he let go but he did it focused on his dick sinking deep into her wet until he could see none of him, none of her, just the two of them together, and he gritted his teeth to drive the beauty of what they had down his throat, his lungs, his gut, his ass, through his balls, out his cock, shooting it in glorious pulsing floods into his Rosalie.

He came down to find she was already down, now fucking herself, and him, on sweet glides.

That was when he moved his hands over her skin, taking her in in a different way, giving her something at the same time.

She made a move as if to draw him out, shift position, and he murmured, "No, honey," and she stilled that movement, but continued to fuck him sweet.

He let her until he lost it and had to slide out completely, but he kept his hands moving on her waist, her lower back, hips, ass, fingertips tracing down the backs of her thighs.

She shivered in front of him and didn't move, quiet, contained, the world that bed and their bodies and Rosalie offering him everything he needed, on her knees, dripping his cum, holding for him, there for him, his world.

"Pete's making a play," he said softly.

"Yeah," she agreed.

"How you feel about that?" he asked, still touching her.

"If she lets it happen, happy for Mom. Thrilled for Big Petey."

He smiled at her back because her words were good.

Renae needed happiness in her life that came from more than her daughter, her daughter's happiness, the relationship she was building with her daughter's man and the Club that man gave them both, and if Pete, who hadn't reached for it himself in years, could give it to her, that worked for Snap.

But he was on the other side, knowing Pete as he did. He'd be happy for Pete if he found someone again. He'd be thrilled for Renae, because she couldn't do better than finding Petey.

The silence settled nice and warm but Rosalie broke it.

"Things are not good."

Yeah, he was right, Rosie had felt it.

"Nope," he confirmed.

"You're all twitchy."

"Yep."

"Anything I can do?" she asked.

"Nope," he answered.

She jerked her head so her hair slid to one side and looked up at him out of the sides of her eyes.

"You sure?"

Laid out, ass up, pussy dripping.

Her invitation was not veiled.

He grinned at her.

"Nope."

She grinned back and wiggled her ass. "Take your time, Mulder."

His drifting fingers slid between her legs. "You better believe it, Scully."

She bit her lip.

He started playing with her clit.

Slowly, his old lady closed her eyes.

And nothing penetrated, not rival bike clubs, not dealing, pimping psychopaths, not what was left for them on that picnic table, not the shift happening in the Club.

The world was small.
In the scheme of things, tiny.
Just Snapper and his Rosalie.
But it was about to crack open.
Open wide.
Sucking them all into a dark void of insanity.

* * * *

It was raining hard.

He was soaked.

His throat was choked.

His hair was straggling in his eyes, eyes that were blinking away the hair and the wet.

And the blood.

His hands were in fists, including the one with its fingers curled around the butt of his gun.

And Everett "Snapper" Kavanagh stared.

This was it.

The end was near.

And by what he was right then seeing, what had just been done, something that had already been hideously nasty was going to get seriously...fucking...ugly.

The red staining the rainwater was pooling at his boots.

It was Black again.

The asshole had tried to pull the same thing on Snap that his mentor had succeeded in doing to Black.

Take out the brother that everyone liked. The even-keeled one.

The calm in the storm.

Take out the brother that would light a fire under the whole Club that was already a powder keg in an attempt not to blow it sky high, but to force them to scramble to put the light out then toe the line.

But this time, seriously fucking fortunately, they'd failed.

"I am the master of my fate," he whispered, head unbowed, blood and water and sweat mingling as it trickled down his neck, into his cut, drenching his tee, the adrenaline that had suffused him as the life he wanted to share with Rosie nearly went black on the stroke of a blade, staring, damned staring, unable to tear his eyes away. "I am the captain of my soul."

It took a lot but he broke eye contact and walked away, sliding up the safety and shoving his gun in the back waistband of his jeans before pulling out his phone, ignoring the pizza he was picking up for him and Rosalie, moving to his truck.

He had to make decisions, and fast.

He made them.

Fast.

So his first call was Rush.

His second call was Throttle.

His third call was Tack.

His last call was Rosalie.

The End

* * * *

Also from 1001 Dark Nights and Kristen Ashley, discover Rock Chick Reawakening.

Sign up for the 1001 Dark Nights Newsletter
and be entered to win a Tiffany Key necklace.

There's a contest every month!

Go to www.1001DarkNights.com to subscribe.

As a bonus, all subscribers will receive a free copy of
Discovery Bundle Three
Featuring stories by
Sidney Bristol, Darcy Burke, T. Gephart
Stacey Kennedy, Adriana Locke
JB Salsbury, and Erika Wilde

Discover 1001 Dark Nights Collection Five

Go to www.1001DarkNights.com for more information

BLAZE ERUPTING by Rebecca Zanetti
Scorpius Syndrome/A Brigade Novella

ROUGH RIDE by Kristen Ashley
A Chaos Novella

HAWKYN by Larissa Ione
A Demonica Underworld Novella

RIDE DIRTY by Laura Kaye
A Raven Riders Novella

ROME'S CHANCE by Joanna Wylde
A Reapers MC Novella

THE MARRIAGE ARRANGEMENT by Jennifer Probst
A Marriage to a Billionaire Novella

SURRENDER by Elisabeth Naughton
A House of Sin Novella

INKED NIGHT by Carrie Ann Ryan
A Montgomery Ink Novella

ENVY by Rachel Van Dyken
An Eagle Elite Novella

PROTECTED by Lexi Blake
A Masters and Mercenaries Novella

THE PRINCE by Jennifer L. Armentrout
A Wicked Novella

PLEASE ME by J. Kenner
A Stark Ever After Novella

WOUND TIGHT by Lorelei James
A Rough Riders/Blacktop Cowboys Novella®

STRONG by Kylie Scott
A Stage Dive Novella

DRAGON NIGHT by Donna Grant
A Dark Kings Novella

TEMPTING BROOKE by Kristen Proby
A Big Sky Novella

HAUNTED BE THE HOLIDAYS by Heather Graham
A Krewe of Hunters Novella

CONTROL by K. Bromberg
An Everyday Heroes Novella

HUNKY HEARTBREAKER by Kendall Ryan
A Whiskey Kisses Novella

THE DARKEST CAPTIVE by Gena Showalter
A Lords of the Underworld Novella

Discover 1001 Dark Nights Collection One

Go to www.1001DarkNights.com for more information

FOREVER WICKED by Shayla Black
CRIMSON TWILIGHT by Heather Graham
CAPTURED IN SURRENDER by Liliana Hart
SILENT BITE: A SCANGUARDS WEDDING by Tina Folsom
DUNGEON GAMES by Lexi Blake
AZAGOTH by Larissa Ione
NEED YOU NOW by Lisa Renee Jones
SHOW ME, BABY by Cherise Sinclair
ROPED IN by Lorelei James
TEMPTED BY MIDNIGHT by Lara Adrian
THE FLAME by Christopher Rice
CARESS OF DARKNESS by Julie Kenner

Also from 1001 Dark Nights

TAME ME by J. Kenner

Discover 1001 Dark Nights Collection Two

Go to www.1001DarkNights.com for more information

WICKED WOLF by Carrie Ann Ryan
WHEN IRISH EYES ARE HAUNTING by Heather Graham
EASY WITH YOU by Kristen Proby
MASTER OF FREEDOM by Cherise Sinclair
CARESS OF PLEASURE by Julie Kenner
ADORED by Lexi Blake
HADES by Larissa Ione
RAVAGED by Elisabeth Naughton
DREAM OF YOU by Jennifer L. Armentrout
STRIPPED DOWN by Lorelei James
RAGE/KILLIAN by Alexandra Ivy/Laura Wright
DRAGON KING by Donna Grant
PURE WICKED by Shayla Black
HARD AS STEEL by Laura Kaye
STROKE OF MIDNIGHT by Lara Adrian
ALL HALLOWS EVE by Heather Graham
KISS THE FLAME by Christopher Rice
DARING HER LOVE by Melissa Foster
TEASED by Rebecca Zanetti
THE PROMISE OF SURRENDER by Liliana Hart

Also from 1001 Dark Nights

THE SURRENDER GATE By Christopher Rice
SERVICING THE TARGET By Cherise Sinclair

Discover 1001 Dark Nights Collection Three

Go to www.1001DarkNights.com for more information

Discover 1001 Dark Nights Collection Four

Go to www.1001DarkNights.com for more information

ROCK CHICK REAWAKENING by Kristen Ashley
ADORING INK by Carrie Ann Ryan
SWEET RIVALRY by K. Bromberg
SHADE'S LADY by Joanna Wylde
RAZR by Larissa Ione
ARRANGED by Lexi Blake
TANGLED by Rebecca Zanetti
HOLD ME by J. Kenner
SOMEHOW, SOME WAY by Jennifer Probst
TOO CLOSE TO CALL by Tessa Bailey
HUNTED by Elisabeth Naughton
EYES ON YOU by Laura Kaye
BLADE by Alexandra Ivy/Laura Wright
DRAGON BURN by Donna Grant
TRIPPED OUT by Lorelei James
STUD FINDER by Lauren Blakely
MIDNIGHT UNLEASHED by Lara Adrian
HALLOW BE THE HAUNT by Heather Graham
DIRTY FILTHY FIX by Laurelin Paige
THE BED MATE by Kendall Ryan
PRINCE ROMAN by CD Reiss
NO RESERVATIONS by Kristen Proby
DAWN OF SURRENDER by Liliana Hart

Also from 1001 Dark Nights

Tempt Me by J. Kenner

About Kristen Ashley

Kristen Ashley was born in Gary, Indiana, USA and nearly killed her mother and herself making it into the world, seeing as she had the umbilical cord wrapped around her neck (already attempting to accessorize and she hadn't taken her first breath!). Her mother said they took Kristen away, put her Mom back in her room, her mother looked out the window, and Gary was on fire (Dr. King had been assassinated four days before). Kristen's Mom remembered thinking it was the end of the world. Quite the dramatic beginning.

Nothing's changed.

Kristen grew up in Brownsburg, Indiana and has lived in Denver, Colorado, the West Country of England and now resides in the Valley of the Sun. Thus, she's blessed to have friends and family around the globe. Her family was (is) loopy (to say the least) but loopy is good when you want to write. They all lived together on a very small farm in a small farm town in the heartland. She grew up with Glenn Miller, The Everly Brothers, REO Speedwagon and Whitesnake (and the wardrobes that matched).

Needless to say, growing up in a house full of music, clothes and love was a good way to grow up.

And as she keeps growing, it keeps getting better.

You can find more information about her books at www.kristenashley.net.

Discover More Kristen Ashley

Rock Chick Reawakening
A Rock Chick Novella
By Kristen Ashley

From *New York Times* bestselling author, Kristen Ashley, comes the long-awaited story of Daisy and Marcus, *Rock Chick Reawakening*. A prequel to Kristen's *Rock Chick* series, *Rock Chick Reawakening* shares the tale of the devastating event that nearly broke Daisy, an event that set Marcus Sloane—one of Denver's most respected businessmen and one of the Denver underground's most feared crime bosses—into finally making his move to win the heart of the woman who stole his.

Wild Like the Wind
Chaos Series
By Kristen Ashley
Coming Summer 2018

Prologue
You'll Never Be Alone

Seventeen years ago…

"Do you have anything to say?"

Hound stood in the line with his brothers of the Chaos Motorcycle Club, staring at the man kneeling before them, waiting for him to say something just so they could end this.

There were four drums of fire dancing at the corners of the grouping. Outside of the moon, that fire was the only thing lighting the clearing. It danced on the man in front of them and on the pine trees surrounding him.

There was nothing but nature out there for miles all around.

And no sound but the fire crackling and the men who were talking.

"Go fuck yourself," the man on his knees spat, literally. The words coming out of his mouth included spittle that Hound could see, even by firelight, was tinted with blood.

His face was a mangled mess because he'd been held with his arms behind his back while each brother took a one-two punch, every one of them packed with power, all the power they could muster.

And with their motivation, they'd each been able to pack a lot of power.

Hound was the only one who'd snuck in a third punch, right to the kidneys.

It was the first but not the last time the man had chucked up blood.

His eyes were swelling shut, his mouth dripping blood, the flesh on his cheeks opened up.

His condition meant he was listing. On his knees because he was forced there, keeping his position probably because he didn't have the strength to get up.

This wasn't about the beating he'd taken from his ex-brothers.

It was that he'd taken the slice of each brother's blade carved deep through his back.

This was Tack's idea, and Hound and every brother that stood with him supported it.

It was about obliterating their mark on his back that claimed him brother.

In the rare event a man renounced the Club, he blacked out the Chaos tattoo inked on his back.

If a man played traitor to the brotherhood, by the brothers' hands that tat would be scorched off.

This man in front of them had not renounced the Club.

He had not simply played traitor to it.

He'd betrayed it in a way none of them would have expected.

A way none of them could allow to go unavenged.

He'd stabbed a brother in the back, figuratively.

But that brother was gone all the same, because the man right there on his knees had ordered the hit.

Therefore he'd taken their blades for two reasons.

An eye for Chaos was not for an eye.

It was for your pound of flesh.

Stab Chaos in the back, that's returned.

And then some.

The man kneeling before Hound and all the brothers of the Chaos MC now had a mangled face and a back that was nothing but opened pulp of bloody flesh.

And very soon he would be what he'd made Black.

Gone.

Hound shifted on his feet, impatient, when their new president, Tack, pushed, "That's all you got to say?"

"Suck my dick," the man on his knees replied.

He was known as Crank.

He'd been their president. Their leader. The man who had sworn to honor his brothers. Respect them above all else.

Protect them, even if it meant giving his life to do it.

And for his own greed and pride, not one fucking thing to do with the brotherhood, he'd brought Black low.

Hound's eyes shifted to Tack as he moved closer to Crank.

"You were Chaos, we were you," Tack said quietly.

It took some effort, but Crank hocked up a loogie and spat it at Tack's boots. It didn't hit its mark but it said what he wanted to say.

Hound shifted impatiently again, feeling his jaw tighten.

"You were Black, he was you," Tack continued, speaking low.

Hound felt that in his throat and swallowed hard to wash it away.

"Fuck you," Crank whispered.

"You ordered your own death by ordering his," Tack told him something he had to know, but even if they hadn't made that clear in the proceedings, he knew it before.

What he did could not stand.

Not even out there in the other world, the world not owned and run by Chaos.

But in their world, retribution for what he did was not swift and it had only one end.

"Motherfucker," Crank hissed. "You killed Black, and you fucking know it."

Hound growled, his eyes cutting to Tack to see his jaw go hard, which meant his brother took that in.

All the boys started to get restless.

"*Order the fire!*" Hound bellowed.

"You've been gagging for the gavel since you were a recruit," Crank bit off to Tack. "It was you that put Black where he is."

"We are not what you made us," Tack replied.

"We're outlaws," Crank shot back.

"We are not what you made us," Tack returned.

Crank swung his torso back and asked sarcastically, "Yeah, right, so I'm gonna walk away from this?"

"No. You. Are. Not," Tack stated deliberately, his face changing from pensive to hostile. "Because we're," he leaned in toward Crank, "*outlaws*. But we're also," he leaned farther forward, "*brothers*." He leaned back and took a step away, ordering, "Get to your feet."

"You take out a man down on his knees, it's as pussy as you're gonna make my Club, so I'll make that statement for you since you'll be taking me out on my knees."

"Face your death on your feet," Tack urged.

"Blow me," Crank clipped.

Tack took a moment to study him.

Then he muttered, "Your call."

After that, he walked back, taking his place in the line.

The men went from restless to wired.

Tack felt it and didn't waste any more time. He couldn't. If someone jumped the gun, this would not be what Tack needed it to be, what the brothers needed it to be.

For Tack, it wasn't about one man taking the right to vengeance from the others.

For Tack, it was about one man shouldering the burden of the end of a human being, even if that being was a man as lowdown dirty, useless and an absolute waste of space as Crank.

They would do it as one.

They would do it as a band of brothers.

That was who Kane "Tack" Allen was.

That was where he was guiding Chaos.

"Brother Crank," Tack called out. "You've been found guilty of a crime against the brotherhood, the worst of its kind, the betrayal of a brother. Your patch has been stripped. You'll rot without the mark of Chaos on your back. Your final sentence is execution. You've had your chance to speak. You've got five seconds to take your feet before you meet your maker."

In the end, unable to do it on his knees, Crank struggled up to his feet.

"Ready!" Tack shouted.

All the men lifted their guns and pointed them at Crank.

But when Hound took aim, his focus was not on Crank.

He was looking at Crank, but everything he had in him was focused on Tack.

So the minute the first sound from the first letter came out when Tack boomed, "*Fire!*" Hound was already squeezing the trigger.

It was a nanosecond before any of his brothers, all who did the same, pulled theirs.

But Hound knew it was his bullet that was the first that penetrated Crank.

And it did this right through his eye.

This made Hound happy.

*****

Later that night, which was the early hours of the morning, Hound was with Tack when they went to the house. He was one of five men with him—Hop, Boz, Dog, Brick, and Hound. They were all, Hound knew, in consideration for being Tack's lieutenants.

For Hound, who was young, this consideration was an extreme honor.

Still.

Hound did not want this.

He had another position in the Club, now more than ever.

And he needed to be free to focus on it.

But he went anyway.

He had to.

For him, there was no other choice.

Tack knocked on the door and she didn't make them wait. She probably hadn't slept in weeks. But she'd know to be waiting for this.

Because she was Chaos.

When she opened it, Hound felt the sight of her hit him like a punch in the throat.

It wasn't about her beauty, which was extreme.

A sheet of black hair that glistened like silk. Lush features that stamped plain her American lineage was either native or seriously exotic. Body, long and lean. Tits, firm and high. Ass, round and sweet. Skin, smooth and tanned.

Hound had rounded the Compound years ago in order to dump a spent keg back there and caught Black fucking his then fiancé, now widow, against the back wall. Before he'd backed away silently, he'd seen that beautiful face in orgasm and he'd never forgotten it.

But it was before that when he'd taken the fall for Keely Black.

So now it was not about her beauty, that punch in the throat.

Now it was about the dead in her eyes, the grief carved in her features in a way each brother knew, Hound especially with the attention he'd given her, she'd not put the effort in to smoothing it out.

She'd met, fallen in love with, married and given two sons to the only man on earth that was good enough for her.

Now he was dead.

And she might be breathing, but she was the same.

"Where are the boys, honey?" Tack murmured.

"Asleep," Keely replied, her unusual, low, smooth voice even on that one word slithering through the air like a ripple of velvet.

She knew the drill and moved out of the way as Tack moved in.

Hop, Boz, Dog, Brick and Hound moved in after her. Each man took time with her, stopping, touching her, pressing lips to her forehead, stubbled cheeks to her smooth one.

Not Hound.

He stopped in front of her and looked down into her dark-brown eyes.

She stared up in his.

I'd take his place if I could, he thought.

But he said nothing.

He just followed his brothers and walked into her living room.

Keely followed him, and after Hound stopped by Brick, Tack spoke.

"It's done."

For a second, Hound didn't know if she heard him.

Then she asked, "It is?"

"It is, darlin'," Tack said gently. "Black has been avenged."

He hadn't, Hound thought. *Not yet. Not fully. But he will be.*

"Now what?" Keely asked, and Hound reckoned he was giving her all of his attention, but at that question he realized he was wrong.

"We—" Tack started.

"I don't care about Chaos," she cut him off.

He felt the men beside him draw in breaths, shuffle their feet uncomfortably, because this wasn't just said about the brotherhood. This was said by Keely, who was an old lady but she was so much a part of Chaos, through Black but also just on her own, she'd loved her place in it so huge, it was also like a punch in the gut.

But Hound narrowed his eyes at her, taking in every inch of her, his lungs on fire, his palms itching, his need to go to her, draw her near, pull her close, absorb her pain, make it all okay so overwhelming, he felt his energy leaking out of him with the effort it took to contain it.

"What I wanna know is, now what? Now what for me? For my boys?" she asked.

"We'll take care of you, Keely. Like Black was still with us, until your last breath, Chaos will have your back. You'll get his cut of everything at the store, the garage. The brothers will—"

"You gonna take out the trash?" she asked.

Yes, Hound thought.

Brick waded in. "If that's what you need, baby."

She looked to Brick. "Okay, so who's gonna make my boys chocolate chip and peanut butter pancakes every Sunday morning?"

I will, Hound thought.

"Keely, darlin'—" Tack began.

"And who's gonna drag Dutch's ass outta bed when he's bein' a pain. He's in kindergarten and he hates school so much, I know I'm gonna have a fight on my hands for the next twelve years until he can see the end of it."

I will, Hound thought.

"We'll be there for your boys," Dog said.

It was like Dog didn't speak.

She kept at them.

"And who's gonna bring me a shit ton of ibuprofen when I get period cramps so bad it makes me sick to my stomach and I can't move?" she pushed. "Who's gonna make up the hot water bottle for me and rub my back until they're gone? Who's gonna do that? Tell me, *who?*"

I will, Hound thought.

No one said anything.

But she still wasn't done.

"And who's gonna fuck me breathless, make me come so hard I think the world is ending? Who's gonna give it to me again and again and again, night after night after *night*, just like I like it? *Exactly* like I like it," she bit out.

I will, Hound thought.

"Keely, honey—" Hop tried gently.

"It's not *done*," she spat, leaning toward Tack, her gorgeous face twisting with an agony no woman should be forced to bear. "It'll never be *done*."

"I used the wrong words, darlin', I'm so sorry," Tack whispered.

"How *done* is he?" she demanded to know.

"Very done," Boz answered firmly.

"Who did it?" she asked Boz.

"We all did," Hop answered.

But her eyes went right to Hound.

And he looked right into them.

She knew.

There was a reason he was called Hound.

It started out as a joke, the guys digging into him about his unusual first name.

But with the hell Crank had thrown them into, it became other things.

Loyalty, one.

Stubbornness, another.

Difficult to rein in, and when he got the scent, impossible to hold back, yet another.

Not giving up and going the extra mile until the job was done, the last.

She was an old lady and she'd been around a long time.

But she was Keely, her heart as open and giving as her mouth was smart. She was Black's and she was Chaos's and she loved it like that. She knew every brother down to his soul. Even if they didn't give her that, she watched, she looked after them in any way she could.

She knew.

Because the first part that made Hound a hound was the most important.

"We've lost Black, but you, Dutch and Jagger haven't lost Chaos," Tack told her, and she turned her attention to him.

Hound felt his entire frame tighten when the change started coming over her features, and he felt his brothers experience the same as the air in the room went flat.

"I can't do it," she said quietly.

"You can," Tack said firmly.

"The boys are lost," she whispered, the agony of a woman who'd lost her man melting into something far more difficult to witness.

The anguish of a mother whose boys lost their father.

"We'll keep them steady," Tack vowed.

"I'm—" she cut herself off and swallowed.

"We got you," Tack said gently. "We'll always have you. We'll always be there."

Keely said nothing, she just stared in Tack's eyes like she was waiting for him to clap his hands, she'd wake up, and the nightmare she was living would be over and she could rest in the knowledge it was all a bad dream.

Tack didn't do this because he couldn't.

So she looked away.

"You want me to get Bev over here?" Boz asked.

Bev was Boz's old lady, and Keely and her were tight.

It took visible effort but she looked at him. "No. If I've gotta go it alone, I gotta learn how to do that."

That was when Hound spoke.

"You'll never be alone."

She turned to him.

"You don't get it," she whispered. "He wasn't the other half of me. He didn't complete me. He wasn't my old man. He wasn't my husband. He wasn't a dick I fell on. He wasn't the father of my sons. He was," her voice suddenly got scratchy, "*my life*. He was my reason to get up every day and *breathe*. He's gone and losing that, losing him, I'll always, *always* be alone."

Hound made no reply because he didn't have one but also because he again felt like he'd been punched in the throat.

"We're gonna look after you," Tack told her, and her gaze went to him. "Please, darlin', he'd want it this way, so will you let us look after you?"

She tossed her head and the sheet of her hair glistened in the light by her couch that was the only lamp lit.

"He'd want it that way, you're right. So…yes," she agreed.

"Let me get Bev over here," Boz again suggested.

She looked to him.

Then she nodded.

"Boz, go. Call," Tack ordered then turned to Hop, Dog, Brick and Hound. "Just go. I'll stay until Bev gets here."

Hop, Dog and Brick nodded and moved to Keely.

Hound just moved to the door.

He turned to her and caught her eyes before he walked out.

He had no idea if she read his promise.

But it wouldn't matter.

He was still going to keep it.

On behalf of 1001 Dark Nights,

Liz Berry and M.J. Rose would like to thank ~

Steve Berry
Doug Scofield
Kim Guidroz
Jillian Stein
InkSlinger PR
Dan Slater
Asha Hossain
Chris Graham
Fedora Chen
Kasi Alexander
Jessica Johns
Dylan Stockton
Richard Blake
BookTrib After Dark
and Simon Lipskar

88774775R00121

Made in the USA
Columbia, SC
04 February 2018